DANCING THROUGH LIFE

BOOK TWO

STILL *Dancing*

PATRICIA M. ROBERTSON

Chapter 1

Pastor Joe hated these phone calls most of all. As a minister he was used to all kinds of calls from church members in crisis from a tragic accident, runaway child or an arrest. Those he could handle. These he could not.

He pulled up to the high school, parked his car and walked the all-too-familiar path to the principal's office. Three calls in as many weeks. He was beginning to doubt his decision to enroll Stephanie in St. Luke's Lutheran high school.

"A new school for a new year. Time for a change," he had told his reluctant daughter.

He walked into the office, saw her slouched in a chair, her uniform skirt rolled up way above her knees.

He didn't say a word. Her attitude told him all he needed to know as they exchanged glances. Stephanie defiantly met his eyes as if to say, "See, I told you so." He refused to answer.

"Three detentions in three weeks," the principal stated calmly. "Perhaps St. Luke's is not the right environment for your daughter, Pastor. She clearly doesn't want to be here."

"What did she do this time?"

"Do you want the whole list or just the highlights?"

Pastor Joe paused to consider. "Just give it to me straight."

"Well, besides her general insubordination and refusal to participate in class, she's been caught smoking on school grounds again. In plain sight. It's as if she wants to be kicked out," she stated. "Are you sure this is the right place for her?"

Of course he wasn't sure. He wasn't sure about anything where Stephanie was concerned, but he couldn't tell the principal that. He was a church pastor, after all. He was supposed to know about these things. Why was it so easy to give out advice where his church members were concerned and so hard to accept it for his daughter?

"Let me talk to her."

"Fine. She has three days of detention. Maybe that will give you both time to think about what is best for Stephanie." Mrs. Clark paused before adding with concern in her voice. "I know you only want what is best for her. It's hard raising a daughter alone. Let me know if there is anything we can do to help. Perhaps the school counselor, Mrs. Deming, could help."

"Like I said, I'll talk to Stephanie and let you know."

It hadn't always been like this. Just six years ago she had been a happy eight-year-old, oblivious to any problems in the world as she lived in the supposedly perfect home with the supposedly perfect mom and dad. Then her world had been blown apart by the loss of her mom. Nothing had been the same since then.

Joe looked at his errant daughter and said, "Let's go," much as if he were commanding a puppy. Stephanie picked up her backpack and happily agreed, relieved to get out of the office.

"And roll your skirt back down to a proper length," he added. Again, Stephanie was only too happy to accommodate her father if it meant getting out of there quicker.

"Three days of detention," he mumbled at her as they walked to the car.

"I told you, Dad. They just have it in for me because I'm the minister's daughter – you know, a PK."

"I know about being a PK. You forget, I was one too, and I never got into the kinds of trouble you do. If it's such a problem for you, maybe you need to go to the public high school."

"Maybe I do," Stephanie said defiantly. "I've had enough of all of this phony religious, holier-than-thou freak show."

"Keep this up and you won't be welcome at that freak show. I could always send you to a boarding school."

"You're just looking for an excuse to get rid of me. I am just a problem since mom died, not like your precious Michelle. Why don't you ship both of us off to boarding school so you can bury yourself in your work – the way you always do – without feeling guilty about it."

"Keep up this attitude and I just may do that."

"Fine," Stephanie snapped as she threw her backpack into the car, climbing in the back seat.

"Fine," he responded, then added, "You know you can sit in the front."

"And talk to you? I'd rather die. I'll sit in the back like the prisoner I am."

"Fine," Joe repeated and started the car. That didn't go well, he thought to himself. Why did she provoke him like that? Why did he let himself be provoked? So like her mother and yet not like her. He didn't know what to do.

Despite the five years since his wife's death, he still felt like he was only half living, like he were in this state of limbo where he existed, nothing more. He who had helped so many grieving families had no ability to help his own. He had given up his position as pastor to a large congregation in an equally large city for a smaller congregation, all within one year of her death, something he had repeatedly told others not to do.

"Don't do anything drastic for the first year after a loss," he always advised. "Don't sell your home and move. Right now your home might feel like it is too painful to live in with the constant reminders of all you had lost, but a year from now those memories that haunt you may be precious reminders of your loved one."

He couldn't bear to live in that rectory with all of its memories, some good, more bad. He couldn't bear another casserole prepared by well-meaning church members and the single women in his church coming over, befriending his daughters, offering to help in the hope of winning him. Or even worse, the ones with pity in their eyes. He hated that he was now considered a desirable catch. He knew the lie of it. He was not a great catch.

A new start in a new town. That was what he had told himself he needed. Away from all the memories. A smaller congregation where no one knew him, with less responsibilities, a quiet town where he could raise his daughters in peace. Yes, there were still the single women, hoping to catch the new single man, but he ably rebuffed each of them, burying himself in his church work. He knew he didn't deserve love. He kept his distance behind a wall of his own making.

The girls had seemed to adapt to the move with little problem, at least at first. Stephanie had been ten at the time, Michelle seven. Both young enough to idolize their dad. But over time problems had started at school. Joe had been hopeful that the move from middle school to high school would have given Stephanie a chance to break out of the pattern she had established. Apparently not, as evidenced by the latest phone call.

Stephanie had stormed out of the car the minute he pulled into the driveway, heading into the house. Now would have been a good time to have another parent around, he thought, one who could head her off at the pass, stop her before she barricaded herself in her bedroom with music blaring. One who could play good cop to his bad cop. Now is when she could use a mother, but all she had was him.

"Wait, young lady. You're not going anywhere until I talk to you," he called after her.

She stopped in her tracks. "So talk," she said.

"Not here, wait till we get inside."

"Yes, that's right. We can't let any church member see that you have a less than perfect family." Now that had hurt. So much like her mother. Did she have any idea how much she was like her mother, he wondered. He followed her into the rectory, greeted the housekeeper then sat her down in the living room. He brushed his hand through his hair as he tried to figure out what to say. A woman's perspective would have been nice right then.

"So talk, Dad," Stephanie crossed her arms in front of her. Just then the phone rang. The housekeeper interrupted them.

"Pastor, it's for you. It sounds like an emergency."

Joe looked over at Stephanie and paused before saying, "I have to take this." He was quietly relieved at the reprieve from his parenting duties. "I'll be back in a minute."

"Sure you will, Dad. Take all of the time you need. You always do anyway. I'll be in my room," Stephanie said as she left the room.

Joe paused for just a minute, torn between his responsibilities as a parent and his responsibilities as a pastor. The pastor in him won out. After all, he knew what to do there.

"Pastor, it's Dale Reese. Can you come to the hospital? Something has happened to Joy."

"Is she all right?"

"We don't know. She collapsed while dancing. It appears to be a broken bone. We are waiting for x-ray results." Joe took down the necessary information.

"I'll be right there," he said, putting down the phone and giving instructions to the housekeeper before leaving.

"Stephanie, I'm going to the hospital. I'll talk to you when I get back." Stephanie didn't hear him as she listened to music through her head phones.

Chapter 2

"He's on his way," Dale said, putting the phone back down. He sat next to Joy as they waited in the emergency room. She was in hospital garb, lying on the bed, clearly in pain. Still she smiled and reassured him.

"You shouldn't have bothered the pastor. He has plenty more important things to do than babysit me at the hospital."

"Humor me. You may not need him but I do." Dale did need someone. He had hated that phone call summoning him to the hospital.

"Dale, Joy fell. We don't know what's wrong. We've called the ambulance," his mother had said.

"I'll be right there."

"Just meet us at the hospital. The ambulance will get here before you do. No sense in you running both places."

Dale beat the ambulance to the hospital. It had been determined that her life wasn't in immediate danger so they had come at a normal speed, with Esther, his mom, following behind in her car.

Dale relived the events of the past year as he waited. It had been a good year. Joy had been cancer-free all year. After the scare during her pregnancy with Grace, everything had settled back into some semblance of normalcy. Still every time the phone rang, every time Joy caught a cold, the fear of what could be, returned. He still couldn't completely free himself of his fear that the cancer might return.

Arriving by ambulance, Joy got assigned a room quicker than walk-ins. Dale was notified of her arrival as his mom came into the waiting room.

"Is Joy here?" she asked.

"They just got here. They're getting her settled. Once she's in a room we'll be able to go back and see her. Who's watching the kids?"

"Kathleen. I told her I would call as soon as I knew anything."

"What happened?"

"We don't know. She was warming up, getting ready for class when we heard her call out."

"Did the kids see her fall?

"No, thankfully they were playing in the office. Ashley hadn't gotten off the bus from school yet. Kathleen was going to get her off the bus, then take them home. Jacob saw her before the paramedics arrived. She talked to him for a moment before they loaded her into the ambulance."

"Did he seem okay?"

"As far as I can tell." They sat in silence for a few minutes. Dale bounced his leg nervously.

"Do you think . . .?" he began.

"No sense in borrowing trouble," Esther stopped him before he could go any further. "We'll know soon enough."

They were called back into the small curtained rooms where Joy lay. Once assured Joy was okay, Esther called Kathleen to check on the kids.

"They're okay," Esther assured Dale and Joy when she hung up. She waited with Dale while Joy went for x-rays. When Joy came back, Esther left to spell Kathleen with the kids.

"Call me as soon as you know anything."

"You'll be the first one I call," he assured her. Joy had been given some pain meds and was floating in and out of consciousness. That was when he had called his pastor.

Dale was relieved to see Pastor Joe. There was something about his presence that helped. He drew strength from this man, not that much older than him but still old enough to serve as a mentor or the big brother he had never had.

During high school he had attended the large evangelical church that Joy and her parents attended, primarily because they had the best youth group in town. His mom had joined him, dragging his sister, Kathleen, along in the hopes she would get some benefit from the youth group. That had not happened but Esther had found spiritual sustenance for herself from attending and so had continued attending once Dale outgrew youth group.

Sometime during his twenties, Dale had started longing for something different. He had done several plumbing jobs for the local Lutheran church and struck up a friendship with their pastor. He felt drawn to a smaller community, especially as he considered marriage and having a family. While a mega church had been good during his teens, a smaller community of families of all ages appealed to him as an adult. Pastor Mike was like a father to him, so once he was married it seemed like the natural thing to start attending St. Luke's. The service with all of the liturgical elements that were foreign to him, grew on him over time, as well as the periods of quiet, something uncommon in the evangelical tradition he was used to. Joy had wanted to be married by her pastor in her home church and so they had the wedding there. Her parents were still active members and they joined them at times, maintaining contact with friends there, but for the most part, Joy had made the transition to the Lutheran church as well, followed by Dale's mother.

"What place is there for me at New Beginnings with all those young people? I feel lost there. At St. Luke's I'm part of the family," she had said when she started attending.

Dale had liked Pastor Mike and was sad to see him retire. "I had hoped you would be around to baptize all my babies," he had told him at his retirement party. Pastor Mike had embraced him warmly and told him he would not be a stranger, even though he knew it was a lie. Once leaving a pastorate it wasn't good to hang around. You had to give the new pastor a chance to bond with the people. He and Dale both knew this. Perhaps after a few years, once a new pastor was firmly established, they would get together for coffee.

"Besides, I'll still need a good plumber," he had added.

After a year with an interim, Dale had been ready for a new pastor. He had been a little unsure about this man still in his prime. As a small church, they tended to either receive ministers freshly ordained or close to retirement. Ministers Joe's age tended to serve in the larger churches in the bigger cities. There was some talk before he came, always was talk and speculation whenever there was a new pastor. Said he was newly widowed.

"Chances are he won't stay long," one church leader had grumbled. "We don't want him coming for a few years while he gets his life together, then abandoning us for a larger church," he complained. Others were more compassionate. The divorced, widowed and single women of the church were intrigued at first, then disappointed as Joe showed no inclination to encourage their advances. And besides, he came with baggage, two daughters.

Joe had settled into the church rectory with his daughters and set about making himself indispensable, working long hours as if punishing himself for something. His daughters attended the school associated with the church, St. Luke's. Pastor Joe had been a great support the past year during Joy's pregnancy and bout with breast cancer. By the time for their youngest, Grace, to be baptized, he had been warmly accepted as part of the family. Dale had been happy to have Grace baptized by this pastor and friend.

Joy was dosing when Pastor Joe arrived. He quietly slipped into the room.

"How is she doing?" he whispered.

"Okay, I guess."

"Do they know what the problem is?"

"Not yet."

"You don't have to whisper. I can hear you," Joy interrupted them. She smiled softly, her eyes still shut.

Pastor Joe reached for her hand. Joy opened her eyes slightly. "I'm sorry Dale bothered you. It's probably nothing. I'm just losing my balance. Seems I slipped while going through my warm-ups."

"It's no bother. I'm happy to be here." Just then a doctor came into the room.

Dale was taken aback when one of the doctors from Joy's oncologist's practice came into their room. This did not bode well, he thought. While not her doctor, they recognized him from the practice. He had filled in at times when her doctor was unavailable. They shook hands. The doctor looked over at Joe.

"And this is . . .?"

"That's our pastor," Dale introduced him. Joe wondered whether to excuse himself after shaking the doctor's hands but when there was no indication by either man that he should leave, he decided to stay, shifting off to the back of the room where he could observe and help if necessary but not get in the way.

"Joy," Dale woke her up, lightly touching her cheek, "the doctor is here."

Joy opened her eyes and tried to sit up when she winced from pain.

"Don't sit up," the doctor told her. "It appears you have broken your hip."

"But how? I wasn't doing anything different from any other day. I didn't fall, didn't twist my hip in any way."

"Yes, well that is the problem. It appears your cancer has metastasized, spreading to your hip, weakening your bones. That's why your hip broke."

"But she was doing so well. No pain – right, Joy? No sign of anything being wrong," Dale said.

"Have you been experiencing any pain or discomfort prior to this?"

"Well, just a little. I thought I was out of shape from the summer. Nothing major."

"It's not uncommon for this to happen. Cancer can be very deceptive. It can show up and grow for months with no symptoms until there is a break, as happened in your case. Other times there may be pain alerting us that something is wrong. Sometimes there is pain and no evidence of cancer growth. It's different for each person," the doctor explained.

Joy laid there only half understanding. "It couldn't be, can't be," she said. "I was doing so well."

"We'll have to do some more tests to confirm the presence of metastasis and the extent of the presence, but it appears your hip is broken. We'll know more after we get the other test results. We'll be admitting you into the hospital for the night while we schedule the tests and determine whether surgery is necessary. Your own doctor will be in to see you tomorrow." The doctor looked back and forth between Dale and Joy then over to Joe.

"Any questions?" he paused, giving them some time for the information to sink in. When they didn't respond he continued. "We are seeing about getting you a room upstairs right now. I'll also have the nurse bring you in some information about bone metastasis."

"What does this mean?" Dale asked, finally starting to wrap his brain around what was said.

"We won't know until all the tests are done."

"But, her cancer is back?"

"It appears to be the case. Most likely this is not bone cancer but breast cancer that has spread to the bone. The prognosis for such cases is better than with bone cancer," the doctor said, pausing to make notations on his clipboard.

The doctor shook Dale's hand before leaving. "As I said, we won't know till we get the test results." He looked at Joy and added, "In the meantime, we will keep you comfortable. Your doctor should be able to tell you more tomorrow." Dale sat with a dazed look on his face.

"But she was doing so much better," Dale finally said.

"We don't know yet, as the doctor said. Maybe it's just a minor set-back," Joe tried to reassure both of them. "Sometimes not knowing can be worse than when you finally find out. Too easy for worse-case scenarios to take over," Joe added knowing too well that telling them not to worry would be to no avail. Still he said it anyway. "Try not to worry, if that's possible."

Just then a nurse and orderly came into the room.

"Looks like you will be staying with us, Mrs. Reese," the nurse smiled at Joy. "We're going to take you upstairs to floor six. Your nurse up there will give you the information the doctor had mentioned. Is there anything else I can get for you before we move you?"

Joy looked over at Dale with a look of fear in her eyes.

"I'll be right here," Dale said, taking her hand. "No," he told the nurse. "We are all set for now."

"Did you want me to come up with you?" Joe asked.

Dale looked over at Joy then back to his pastor.

"No," he said, "You've already done enough just by coming. You've got family to get home to. We'll be okay for now."

"Let me know if I can do anything more," Joe said taking Joy's hand in his.

"Just pray, Pastor," Joy said quietly.

"That I am," he stated, whispering a quick prayer under his breath as the bed rolled away.

"Thank you," Dale said as he shook Joe's hand then followed after his wife down the glaring hallway.

Joe left the hospital feeling unsure of himself. He felt so ineffective. What was there to say in the face of cancer in one so young? Despite his years of training and experience, he still felt helpless and inadequate in the face of such tragedy. His problems with Stephanie paled in comparison. He had forgotten about this while in the emergency room. Now that he was on his way home, they were returning with full force.

What was he to do, he asked himself as he tried to clear his head enough to deal with the problem at hand. What to do about

Stephanie? Maybe it was time to call her bluff. If she clearly isn't happy at St. Luke's, maybe it was time for a real change.

Chapter 3

"Have you heard anything?" Esther asked as soon as she arrived at Dale and Joy's.

"No, I was hoping you had some information. How is Joy?" Kathleen asked.

"Don't know. I left shortly after she arrived. I know you have to work tonight. Dale is with her. I figured I was needed here more than at the hospital. How are the kids?"

"They seem to be okay. A little worried but easily distracted. Ashley was upset when I met her but got over it." Kathleen paused before adding, "She's up to something."

"Why do you say that?"

"I caught her sneaking out behind the shed when we got home. I couldn't go see what she was up to because I couldn't leave Jacob and Grace. You want me to go look now?"

Esther looked at the clock. "No, it's already five o'clock. Don't you have to be at work at six?"

"Yes, but it will only take a minute." Kathleen was more curious than concerned.

"I'm sure it's nothing. And if it is something, it can wait. We've had enough surprises for one day."

"Okay," Kathleen reluctantly agreed. She gave the kids kisses before taking off. "I close tonight," she reminded her mom. "I might go out with some friends after work so don't worry if I'm not home right away," she added.

Don't worry, like that would happen, Esther thought. Since when did she not worry where her kids were concerned?

"Don't stay out too late. Don't you have class tomorrow?" she said, biting her tongue.

"Mom, I'm not a kid any more. I can take care of myself," Kathleen said as she went through the door.

"You'll always be my kid," Esther said to the closing door. Now what was Kathleen up to, she wondered.

It seems the honeymoon was over. Kathleen had worked at McDonald's for six months before graduating to Pizza Hut. She had proven that she could be reliable; she kept regular hours and had a good job record, which had translated into a new position. Not that Pizza Hut wasn't still fast food, but Kathleen had been ready for a change. She was waiting tables and making more with her tips than she had made at McDonald's. The down-side though was that she had to work evenings and weekends, cutting into her time with her sons, Josh and Scott. Still, they appreciated the pizza she brought home for late-night snacks and breakfast and packed for school lunches. And with her employee discount she even bought hot pizza for dinner now and then. How those boys could eat so much pizza she didn't know. Hollow legs they had, with an insatiable craving for all things pepperoni.

Kathleen had been doing so well at McDonald's. She had even started dating a former classmate, Jack Trimble. He was a CPA and had his own accounting firm. Kathleen couldn't have done much better. Esther didn't know what happened.

"What happened to that nice accountant you were dating?" she had asked last summer.

"Him, oh, he's still around," Kathleen had answered.

"How come we never see him anymore?"

"Mom, we are just friends. He's not my type."

"Then what is your type? He seemed nice enough, had a steady job, a business leader in the community."

"I'll know when I see it."

"You're not dating one of those troublemakers from high school."

"Mom, I hardly have time to sleep between school, work, the kids and helping out at Joy's. When would I find time for trouble?" Kathleen had playfully answered.

Esther hadn't believed her then and believed her even less now. Kathleen didn't have to go looking for trouble. It usually found her. Recently she had started going out after her shift at Pizza Hut. Esther didn't know where she went and with whom, but she suspected she was up to no good.

"Nothing good happens after midnight," she had remarked to her dad.

"On the contrary, I can remember some pretty fine nights after midnight, staying out with my friends, staying up with your mom, dancing until the dance hall closed then talking until the sun rose."

"That's different, and you know it, Dad."

"I'm just saying, why borrow trouble? Kathleen's kept her nose clean for the past year. She's working, going to school. She's still young. Let her have some fun with her friends. I'm glad she's finally doing more than hanging out here with us old farts."

"Speak for yourself."

"You know what I mean," and she did. It's just with Kathleen she never felt like she could completely let down her guard. There were all those years of history to overcome. This past year had been the longest time without trouble where Kathleen was concerned, if you don't count the years in prison when she was someone else's concern, which she didn't. She was waiting for the other shoe to drop.

Dale called shortly after Kathleen had left to let her know Joy would be spending the night in the hospital.

"How is she?"

"The doctor says she broke her hip."

"But how could she? She was only doing warm-ups."

"Well, that's just it. It wasn't the warm-up exercises. Seems her cancer has metastasized to the bone, making it porous. It didn't take much for the break."

"What?" Esther sat down at the kitchen table.

"It looks like the cancer has spread to her bones. The doctor wants to run some more tests to be sure and see if it has spread any farther than her hips."

"That's bad," Esther said softly.

"Well, it isn't good news. We'll know more tomorrow."

"Did you want me to stay overnight?"

"No, I'll stay here with Joy for a while longer then come home. They've got her on a lot of pain meds because of the break. She's been dosing off and on. I'll stay until she is settled for the night, probably nine or so."

"Okay, let me know if you need anything else from me."

"Thanks, Mom. I know. We can always count on you, always have. Watching the kids is huge. We both appreciate it."

"If a grandma can't watch her grandkids now and then, she's not much of a grandma, is she?"

"You go above and beyond, Mom. I'll see you later."

"What do I tell the kids?"

"Tell them Mommy's okay and I'll be home later."

"And if anyone calls?"

"Anyone else can wait."

"What about Joy's parents?"

"I'll call them. Thanks, Mom."

"Is Mommy all right?" Esther jumped when she heard Jacob behind her.

"She's okay."

"Then why isn't she home?" She wasn't sure how much he had seen at the studio. Joy had reassured him as she was being carried out by the paramedics.

"Mommy is fine, Jacob," she had told him. "I'm just going with these nice men to the hospital to be checked out. You stay here with Grandma and Aunt Kathleen. I'll be home soon," she said as she kissed him goodbye. Esther had had to pull him away.

"The doctors want her to stay overnight. Your dad will be home later."

"I want to see Mommy now."

"I know honey. That's not possible right now. Do you want to help me make dinner?"

"No," he pouted.

"Then how about you sit here while I finish up. Where's Ashley?"

"I don't know." Esther remembered what Kathleen had said. Did she dare leave Grace and Jacob to look for Ashley? Just then Ashley came inside.

"Where have you been?" she asked.

"Outside."

"Outside where? And where is your coat?"

"Grandma, can you keep a secret?"

"That depends on the secret."

"I need some help."

"With what?"

"With Muffin." Ashley led her out the back door, down the porch steps. Under the steps was a mangy mutt.

"Ashley, where did this dog come from?"

"I found him out by the shed yesterday. He was cold and needed a place to stay."

"Why didn't you tell your dad?"

"Because he would have taken him away. I've been trying to bring him food and water but he's still hungry. Can I keep him, Grandma?"

"That's not for me to say, Ashley, you know that. It's up to your mom and dad. Besides, he may belong to someone." The stray was a brown, brindle color, at least as far as she could see under the coat of mud. He had a lab's body, with a scrunched-in face like a bull dog, one only a mother and a small child could love. Clearly a mutt.

"A dog," Jacob shouted with delight as he looked over the porch railing.

"Jacob, get back inside. Where is your coat, young man?"

"Please, Grandma, can I keep him?"

"You have to ask your mom and dad."

"Please, Grandma," Jacob chimed in. The dog looked up with big brown eyes as if pleading as well.

"He's probably starving. The least we can do is feed him." Esther paused to figure out what they could give him.

"Our neighbors got a dog. Maybe they'll give us some dog food," Ashley suggested.

"He can have my dinner," Jacob added. "I'm not hungry."

"That's okay. We'll think of something. We can't have you go hungry, too. I'll see what I can do. You two go inside and get ready for dinner."

"Not without Muffin."

"Who said his name was Muffin?" Jacob argued.

"I found him, I get to name him."

"There's no naming the dog," Esther interrupted. "He probably already has a name and an owner that's looking for him." She went inside and returned with some hot dogs.

"Come on boy," she lured him out with the hot dogs. She saw he had a collar but no tags. She managed to lure him up the porch steps and into the mud room. "We have to clean him up before he comes in."

"I'll do it, Grandma," Ashley ran to the bathroom and returned with a wash cloth, a basin of water and a towel.

"Not your mom's good towels, Ashley," Esther started to say. Ashley was already slopping water on the dog.

"Let me help too," Jacob insisted. Meanwhile Esther heard Grace crying from the play pen where she had been placed for safe keeping while Esther cooked dinner. She didn't know what to do as things seemed to be getting out of hand. Who could she call on? Kathleen had her dad's car so he couldn't come over and help. Josh didn't have a driver's license yet, or a car. She did what she had done all this past year when life got out of control. She called Peter.

"Peter, I'm at Joy and Dale's. Could you come over?"

Peter heard the urgency in her voice and didn't stop to ask questions.

"I'll be right there."

Just then the dog broke loose from the grip of the two children and ran to the kitchen, lured by the smell of cooking food. When Esther came in to get him, he ran for the living room and shook his wet hair all over the carpet before jumping over the couch.

"Muffin, Muffin," Ashley kept yelling as she ran after him.

"His name's not Muffin," Jacob yelled.

"Is so," Ashley yelled back.

"Then why doesn't he answer to Muffin? It's a girl's name."

"Stop arguing and let's head him off before he runs upstairs," Esther told the kids. "Where is he now?" They heard the crash of a pan coming from the kitchen.

"The kitchen!" Esther shouted. They ran for the kitchen door while Grace laughed and said, "Dog!" repeatedly.

In the kitchen, the dog had managed to knock the spaghetti sauce that had been simmering, off the stove and onto the floor, where he was licking up the mess.

"I guess we don't have to worry about what to feed him anymore. Here, you forgot the noodles," Esther threw some spaghetti noodles on his head as the kids laughed.

"You think this is funny?" Esther asked and proceeded to throw spaghetti at the kids as they continued to laugh.

She managed to grab the dog by the collar and pull him back to the mud room. When Peter arrived she was busy cleaning up the remainder of the spilled spaghetti sauce while Ashley and Jacob attempted to clean sauce out of the dog's fur.

"What's going on here?" he asked as Esther threw spaghetti noodles at him. "So this is the emergency I had to rush across town for." He pretended to be angry.

"Look, Peter, we have a dog," Ashley and Jacob came into the kitchen, holding the dog by the collar.

"Well, if you ask me, that's one lucky dog," Peter stated. At the word lucky, the dog barked.

"Lucky, lucky, are you trying to tell us your name is Lucky?" Peter asked as the dog ran to him.

"I told you his name wasn't Muffin," Jacob told Ashley. "Here boy, here Lucky." At this the dog came back to Jacob.

"So, a pet emergency?" Peter asked.

"Yes, what are we going to do with him? We don't have any dog food for him or a leash or rope to tie him up out back."

"Where's Dale?"

"At the hospital with Joy," Esther pulled him aside to fill him in on the situation. Fortunately the kids were too busy with Lucky to notice. They were calling him by name and leading him through the house.

"What happened?" Peter asked, becoming serious.

"Joy fell at the dance studio. She went by ambulance to the hospital. Seems her cancer has spread to her bones. They don't know how bad it is just yet. They are going to keep her overnight and run more tests. Dale will be home in a while." Esther paused to catch her breath. "What do I do about the dog? Ashley found it yesterday and hid him in the shed out back. I don't know what to do. Dale has enough on his mind without worrying about a dog, but look how happy Ashley and Jacob are. At least he has taken the kids' minds off of their mom. I don't have the heart to take the dog away."

"What do the kids know?"

"Just that their mom fell and is in the hospital. Jacob was at the dance studio when it happened. He was pretty upset."

Peter looked around at the mess, "I think for now we finish cleaning up. I take it this was to be your dinner?"

"Yes, Lucky got away from us and knocked the pan off the stove. He must have been starving."

"Well, we don't have to worry about food for him, at least not tonight. What do you have here to eat that is quick and easy?"

"Hot dogs and boxed macaroni and cheese."

"Fine, why don't you make that and I'll run to the store for dog supplies, food and a leash at least."

"Should we take him to the pound?" Esther asked.

They looked through the door to the living room where Jacob and Ashley were still playing with Lucky, then looked at each other in agreement.

"I guess we'll just have to wait until Dale gets home and explain what happened."

Later that night, while brushing their teeth, Jacob asked, "When is Mommy coming home?" Ashley pretended not to be listening, continuing to brush her teeth, but her ears perked up at the mention of her mother.

"We don't know yet," Esther said, "But your dad will be home soon." She sought to reassure them by this.

"Why can't Lucky sleep in my room?" Ashley whined.

"Because I said so, just get to bed," Esther admonished the two of them. They had already had this conversation. Still she was glad for the change of subject.

Dale was emotionally and physically drained by the time he got home at nine. He wasn't surprised to see Peter's car in the driveway. He knew Peter was dating his mom and had become a frequent guest at their home.

"How's Joy?" they both asked as soon as he came in the door. He told them what little he knew.

"She seems to be resting somewhat peacefully, thanks to the drugs. How are the kids?"

"About the kids …" Esther started. Dale wondered, what now?

"Are they okay?"

"Come see for yourself," Peter said. They went upstairs to Ashley's bedroom where Ashley and Jacob were sharing a bed with Lucky. Neither had been willing to let the other have the dog to themselves. Esther had tried getting them to sleep in their own bed with Lucky in the mud room. First Lucky had howled until let back into the house where he found his way to Ashley's room, then Jacob had snuck into bed with Ashley and Lucky.

"What?" Dale began.

"I'm sorry, Dale. It's my fault. It seems Ashley found him yesterday and hid him in the shed. We cleaned him and fed him. I told them he probably belongs to someone. I just didn't have the heart to take the dog to the pound," Esther said.

"So I get to be the bad guy," Dale started.

"Don't blame your mom. I couldn't do it either. The kids were so happy. What does it hurt to keep him one night?"

"Because in one night they are already attached to the dog and I'll have to take it away."

"Maybe not. Maybe they won't find the owner," Esther said.

"Mom, you know better than that. We can't keep a dog, not with everything with Joy . . ." Dale didn't know whether he was fighting tears of anger or sadness.

"I know, honey. I'll take care of it. You have enough to deal with right now. I'll call the pound and see if anyone lost a dog. I'll tell the kids. I'll come over first thing tomorrow."

"I'm sorry, Mom. I just can't deal with this right now."

"I know, son. I know. Do you want me to take the dog home with me?"

Dale looked at his sleeping kids. "No, let him stay. We can sort this out in the morning." He escorted his mom and Peter out.

"I hope we did the right thing," Esther said to Peter before they went to their separate cars.

"I hope so, too. Time will tell," Peter said as they exchanged a quick kiss and climbed into their cars, driving home exhausted and worried.

Chapter 4

Kathleen thought that last table of customers would never leave.

"What's your hurry? Got a hot date?" the other waitress asked.

"No, just meeting some friends, shooting some pool. You want to join us?"

"You forget, I have a husband and kid waiting for me. I've got to get home."

"One drink wouldn't hurt," Kathleen tempted.

She just laughed, "Maybe another time."

Like that was going to happen, Kathleen thought, Miss "I've got a life to go home to." She had someone to go home to, too, Josh and Scott, but they would be studying or chatting on the internet. They were only too happy to eat her pizza, but after that they had a life of their own. She was only a small part of that life, sitting on the fringe, as befit a mom of two teenagers. Josh was now a junior and Scott a freshman. They had little use for her, typical of high school students. Their lives revolved around their friends.

Her own mom had played little part in her high school years. She remembered those days as a haze of school, sneaking out, getting into trouble, hanging out with friends. She didn't have that many fond memories of those days, which was why she hadn't looked up any of her high school friends when she had returned. Those days were behind her as far as she was concerned. She was trying for a fresh start. That was why dating Jack Trimble had seemed like a good idea at the time. He had been as far removed from her life in high school as if they had been on different planets. She had hung out with the lowlifes, the kids who were always in detention, who barely graduated or flunked out and maybe got a GED. He was one of the geeks at the time. A bit nerdy, he had been a "mathlete" in high school. Numbers were his whole life. She had dealt numbers for a while in Chicago, but not the same numbers.

She had wanted a fresh start once she made her mind up to stay in her hometown. She had considered him a loser at first. Who would have returned after once leaving for college?

"So, why did you return? You're smart, you've got your degree. You could have set up shop just about anywhere. Why come back here?" she had asked on their first date.

"Why not? I had friends here, family, it's not a half bad place to live if you just give it a chance."

So she was giving it and him a chance – but she didn't know why. It just didn't feel right. Her family, especially Dale, had loved Jack.

"I haven't seen Jack much lately. What's he up to?" Dale had questioned her.

"Why should I know?"

"You are dating him, aren't you?"

"No, we broke up a few weeks ago."

"Why? He makes good money. You would have been set for life."

"Maybe I don't want to be set for life. Maybe I want to make it on my own."

"So make it on your own. Who says you can't do that and still have a husband? Look at Joy. She has a successful business and a family."

"Not everyone is as lucky as me," Joy interrupted.

"Besides he has two kids from his first wife," Kathleen explained. "I don't think I would be very good in the role of step mother." The one who had understood had been Joy when they had talked later.

"So what is up with Jack?"

"You know, there was no chemistry. He's a good enough guy but he's kind of . . ."

"Boring?" Joy said.

"Yes, boring. He's like this town, a dead-end with no excitement. It may be good for you, but not for me, no insult intended."

"None taken. I like it here but I can understand wanting something more. There isn't exactly a lot for someone young and single to do here."

"I'm not that young anymore and not getting younger."

"Do you miss Chicago?"

"Yes and no. I don't miss the life I led there, but there were good times. I miss the night life, restaurants, clubs open till all hours."

"We do have a Denny's, open twenty-four hours!" Joy teased.

"And shows. I didn't go to a lot of them, but when I did . . . I loved it. You can't get that here. And the subway. It was so much easier to get around there. Here, if you don't have a car you are stuck."

"Okay, okay. I get your point. So are you going to leave?"

"I don't know. I pretty much promised Josh that I would stay till he graduates, not that he needs me that much."

"Believe me, you are still important to him. Don't misread that high school swagger."

"And I do want to finish my degree." She had another year of classes before she completed her associate's degree and was considering transferring from the community college to a four-year college for her bachelor's.

"So what would make you want to stay?"

"I don't know. Maybe it's not a what but a who."

"Apparently Jack isn't the right who, so who is?"

"Right now it's Josh and Scott. After they graduate there won't be anyone to keep me here."

"Not even your loving brother and me?" Joy teased.

"I don't know. Maybe. I don't think Dale really cares whether I stay or go."

"You'd be surprised. And there's your mom and grandfather."

"Yes, I owe them for all they've done for me and the boys. I guess that's reason for staying. It's just sometimes I feel like I've got to get out or I'm going to go crazy."

"So go out."

"And do what?"

"I'm sure you'll think of something," Joy had said and excused herself. "Time to get some sleep. Grace will have me up before the sun rises."

Kathleen had been ready for something different when she had seen the sign for waitresses at the local Pizza Hut. She had been treating Josh and Scott. On the way out she saw the sign and stopped to read it when Scott said, "Go for it, Mom."

"Go for what?"

"The job. You don't want to work at McDonald's forever, do you? And you get to take home all the mistake pizzas. My friend's brother delivers pizza. He's always bringing home pizza."

She didn't want to work at McDonald's for the rest of her life, even though she had been offered the position of assistant manager. Her boss liked her and could see she was smarter than most of his employees. She turned down the offer and applied for and got the job at Pizza Hut. That had been six months ago. Now she was tiring of this one as well. Then one of her friends from high school showed up.

"Turtle, how are you?" He had been named "Turtle" because of his penchant for turtle-neck shirts back then.

"I'm not Turtle any more. See the polo shirt?"

"You'll always be Turtle to me. So what are you doing?"

"Running my dad's trucking company."

"For real? I thought you hated that place."

"I did, but I like the money it brings in. With a wife and kids, a steady income helps."

"You, married with kids? I can't believe it."

"Believe it. Here are their pictures. That's Melinda and there's Jessica and Todd junior."

"Thank God, they have their mother's looks."

"They also take after their mother in other important ways. They've got their mom's brains, though how I got her to marry me is beyond me. Could have something to do with the fact I knocked her up."

"That could have done it. So what's the rest of the gang up to?"

"Not a lot of us left. The lucky ones left town, like you."

"Sounds to me like you're the lucky one."

"Luckier than I deserve. Hey, why don't you find out for yourself?"

"What do you mean?"

"Some of us are getting together at the Green Door tonight. Remember that place?"

"How could I forget?"

"Come on over when you get out of work."

"I don't know. I've got kids."

"Just a few beers with friends. A chance to talk about the old times. You know where we'll be. Hope to see you there." He said as he left.

"Maybe you will," she replied.

She had called her mom and let her know she would be late. Her friends were older, as was she. It felt good to be with people her own age. What had started as a one-time night out had quickly become a regular part of her life.

Chapter 5

Joy slept fitfully through the night. Reality mixed with dreams so that she didn't know what was true and what was fiction. She vaguely remembered falling, feeling a sharp pain and calling for help. She remembered giving instructions to her assistant. Fortunately last year she had been talked into hiring another dance instructor to help her with her teaching load.

At Esther's suggestions she had added some adult dance classes during the day as well as exercise classes for women recovering from mastectomies. The group had quickly become an additional support group for her. One can never have too many supportive people in your life, Joy told herself, happy to have these women in her life who had faced what she had faced and come through it to the other side. She also was renting space to a yoga instructor to offer classes in the morning. Esther was handling the business aspects of these additions.

The office she had set up for her sister, Sara, last year remained empty. It was used as extra storage space for costumes and ballet slippers before the dance recital and as a quiet refuge for reflection when she needed to get away from the commotion of students coming and going. The picture Sara had painted of her last year remained in a prominent position on the wall outside the door to the office. Sometimes it was an unwelcome reminder of all she had gone through the past year. Joy looked at the woman she had once been, pregnant, hands raised in praise as she balanced in the heavens, dancing on a high wire.

It had been a source of comfort when Sara had given it to her, reminding her of all those who loved her and were praying for her, all those angels in the clouds. Now she wanted to put that part of her life behind her. Still she couldn't bring herself to move the picture that Sara had designed with so much love. Even though its significance had changed for her, it still held significance. She preferred the ink drawings that were displayed on the walls in the office space. She wanted no thought of angels or heaven right now. She had skirted death. Heaven can wait for another time, a much later time.

Esther had talked to her about setting up a gift shop in the space, with cards and books as well as dance and yoga supplies.

"It could be a healing center," Esther had suggested. "We could include inspirational messages for others who have dealt with cancer or other hardships, books on healing and health, maybe even on meditation." Joy let Esther dream. She had big ideas for the building that held the dance studio, ideas that Joy simply didn't have time for while raising her children. Joy wasn't ready to dream that big just yet.

She was grateful now that she had been talked into hiring Leticia as her assistant so she had someone to take over her classes rather than having to cancel them. Leticia had been one of her students. As a teenager she had paid for her classes by helping Joy in the younger classes. Leticia had helped out during Joy's pregnancy with Grace and was a natural choice to hire as assistant while she pursued her studies at college.

Joy remembered seeing Jacob's small face from across the room, the fear in it. She remembered talking to him but not what she had said. She remembered the ride in the ambulance, the sharp pain every time they hit a bump in the road. Then she remembered the emergency room and Dale and some doctor talking to her, saying things she didn't understand, didn't want to understand. Then it seemed she was back in the hospital having Grace and a double mastectomy. It all blended together in her dreams. She cried out for Dale but he wasn't there. Someone was going to take their baby. Someone was going to take all of her babies. Someone was going to cut into her. Where was Dale? She cried out in her sleep then went back into a fitful dose.

"Where am I?" she asked when the nurse turned on the light to take her blood pressure.

"In the hospital."

"Where's my husband?"

"He's on his way." That was all she needed to know. Then she dosed back into sleep. Next time she woke up Dale was sitting next to her just like she knew he would be.

"Where have you been?" she asked with a smile.

"Getting the kids to school. Your mom is watching Grace."

"Is Jacob okay?"

"He seems to be."

"He looked so small and afraid yesterday."

"How are you?" Dale decided to change the subject.

"Okay, I guess. I had the worst nightmares, Dale. I dreamed the doctor said my cancer had come back."

"It wasn't a dream, Joy. It has," Dale stated softly.

"No, it's not possible. I would have known. I would have felt it in my bones. I didn't feel anything."

"The doctor said it can be like that. Cancer can be unpredictable. There can be no sign before a relapse. We'll know more when we talk to your oncologist today."

"It can't be, Dale. I was doing so good. We were doing so good. It can't be, not when we've just gotten our lives back together. This is another nightmare," Joy cried.

"It's real, Joy, but I'm here now. I'm real. I'm here for you and will always be here for you." He held her hand as she cried.

"I just don't know that I can do it again. I can't go through this."

"Yes, you can, and you will. We will do this together. Besides we don't know what we are dealing with yet. Let's wait until we hear from the doctor."

"It's just hard not to imagine the worst." Dale knew full well what Joy was talking about as his brain had entertained those thoughts all night long, depriving him of much-needed sleep.

The nurse paused to give them some time before she came in.

"The doctor doesn't want you having anything to eat or drink until all of the tests are done, in case surgery is necessary. We are going to take Joy for an MRI. Is there anything I can do for you?" she asked Dale.

"No, we're okay," Dale assured the nurse, assuring himself as well. "Didn't that get done yesterday?"

"They did x-rays and a bone scan. This will give him more information."

Dale waited in the room while Joy was taken out for the MRI. He thought about going to work but wanted to be here when Joy got back. He also didn't want to take any chance of missing the doctor when he came.

He had called Joy's parents the night before. They had wanted to rush up to the hospital. He had looked over at Joy and she had shaken her head, no.

"No ... no need to come here tonight. We'll call you tomorrow and let you know what's happening." He had managed to put them off.

"Thank you. I can't deal with my parents just yet," Joy told him.

"I know, but we'll have to deal with them sometime."

"Just not tonight," Joy had said as she dosed off.

Dale and Joy were surprised when the doctor arrived later that morning.

"That was quick," Dale commented. The doctor shook both of their hands, pulling up a chair in order to be face to face with Joy rather than towering over her, before informing them about the test results.

"It appears you have mets in your bones." At the puzzled look on their faces the doctor explained, "Metastases or mets for short."

"So the cancer has come back?" Dale stated hesitantly, not wanting to state what they both feared most.

"The testing can be inconclusive, that's why I ordered the MRI. I also wanted to look for any suspicious spots throughout the rest of the body. The best way to be sure is a biopsy, but it appears that your breast cancer has spread to the bones, specifically to your pelvis area which caused the break."

"That means it is stage IV?" Joy said, bracing herself for the worst.

"Yes, but it's not as bad as it sounds. There is no cure but it can be controlled. Your mets appear to be only in the bones. That's a good sign. It's much easier to control at this stage. I have a number of patients who have been living with mets for years, one over ten years."

Joy felt her body relax as she took in this information. Maybe it wasn't as bad as she had feared, she reassured herself. Dale gripped her hand, giving it a loving squeeze.

"There are several options. First, you do have a hip fracture. We need to address that. You can let it heal naturally. The bone hasn't slipped and it appears to be stable, though we would need to monitor it to make sure it stays that way. We don't put people in a cast for a hip fracture, too difficult. You would need to be in a wheel chair and restrict your movement. We could put cement into the bone to strengthen it." The doctor paused to make sure they were following what he was saying. "We would still need to do a biopsy to be sure about what we are dealing with."

"And the other option?" Dale asked.

"The other option would be hip replacement surgery. Your hip joint is substantially weakened by the mets. We could remove it entirely, thereby getting rid of much of the cancer. The recovery time for hip replacement is actually reasonably quick, quicker than knee replacement surgery. You could be back to full mobility in two or three months. Once we remove the bones we can biopsy them."

"So what's the drawback?" Dale asked.

"There isn't one, except for the slight possibility that the biopsy would show no cancer."

"Meaning we would have had surgery for nothing?" Dale continued.

"Not for nothing. You still had to deal with the fracture."

"What do you think, Joy?" Dale asked.

"Will I have to be in a wheel chair?"

"Maybe, but not likely. They usually try to get patients up and walking right away after surgery. You will be walking with a walker."

"Then that's a no-brainer. Do the hip replacement," Joy said.

"That's what I would recommend."

"How soon can you do it? I can't wait to get out of here and back home."

"We have some fine orthopedic surgeons here. I have already talked to a colleague about your case. He might be able to fit you in later this afternoon if all goes well with his scheduled surgeries. Otherwise he will fit you in tomorrow morning. Other questions?"

"Yes, after the surgery, what then?" Joy asked.

"There were a few other suspicious spots, but all in your bones. Once the biopsy confirms the cancer and after you've had some time to regain your strength, we will put you on meds to control the mets. We'll talk further about that later, for now let's get that hip taken care of and get you back home." He said as he stood up, made some notes and prepared to leave.

"Thank you, doctor," Dale said, standing up himself and shaking his hand. Joy added her thanks.

"No need to thank me. Let's just get you better. That's all the thanks I need."

"Hmmm, meds for mets," Joy commented after he left. Dale's lips smiled, but his eyes remained serious.

They were able to fit her in later that afternoon. He stayed with her the whole time, working on his computer while she slept, talking to her and holding her hand when she was awake.

As they waited for the anesthetic to take effect he mentioned, "By the way, it seems we have a dog."

"What?" Joy would have shot up in bed if not already half way out.

"A dog, the kids found a dog."

"Are you crazy? I'll get you Dale Reese . . ." she said as she fell the rest of the way into a deep drugged sleep.

Chapter 6

Sara couldn't wait to get home and share her big news. It had truly been a "golden" birthday for her. She had turned twenty two on the twenty second of September. Larry had planned well. A golden birthday for a golden year. This had turned out to be the best year ever, especially in light of the previous year, her broken engagement and Joy's cancer. Her move to Detroit had proved to be the right choice. She was sharing an apartment with her college roommate, Anne. Anne had gotten an AmeriCorps position in Detroit. They had a small apartment in a relatively safe area, all they could afford with Anne's limited income and her college loans to pay back.

While her job wasn't everything she had ever dreamed of, it paid the bills and gave her enough money to continue her true passion, art. She was taking classes at the DIA, Detroit Institute of Art, her absolutely favorite place in the city. She routinely slipped off during her lunch hour in order to sit beneath the massive expanse of Diego Rivera's series of frescos in the inner courtyard at the DIA. She knew every aspect of its chronicle of the labor movement.

She was working, creating and preparing for a juried showing of her art come November. It couldn't get better, but it did. Amidst all of this, intertwined, interwoven, undergirding all of the good things happening was her relationship with Larry.

The move to Detroit had been as much about him as her new job, maybe more about him. She had decided to give the relationship a chance by being closer. The move had paid off with dividends. There had been a few bumps in the road, the usual number of misunderstandings as they got to know each other, but overall the relationship had gotten stronger over the year and now this.

Sara looked down at the ring on her finger, turning it around and around, gazing at it from all angles as if she couldn't believe it was there. Where the proposal from Jeff two years ago had been off the cuff, not planned out, Larry had gone out of his way to make it memorable. They had arranged to meet for a long lunch at the DIA, both getting out of work to do so. They went to her favorite spot to look at Rivera's frescos – then, just as she was preparing to get up and return to work, Larry had stopped her.

"Larry, we'll be late getting back to work," she had protested.

"Don't worry. It's all taken care of," he said as he pulled a box out of his pocket. "Our bosses know that if you don't return to work it will be because you said yes," he said as he opened the box. A small diamond sparkled in a simple setting.

"I know it's not much, I mean, not the diamond you deserve, but when we hit twenty-five years you can turn it in for a bigger one."

"Larry, does this mean … ?"

"It means, I'm asking you to marry me. Sara Vanwagon, will you do me the honor of being my wife?"

"Yes, yes I will," Sara said without a moment of hesitation. There was no question in her mind that he was the one for her. She kissed him and heard a ripple of applause. She hadn't noticed the small group that had gathered to witness the proposal; she had been so wrapped up in the moment. In the group were her boss and Larry's boss along with a few co-workers and some stray visitors to the Institute that had happened upon the event.

"She said yes!" Larry shouted to the group. "Sorry, Sara, one of the conditions for getting the afternoon off was that they got to be part of it. You can go back to work now." Larry tried to wave them away.

"Not till I kiss the bride-to-be," Larry's boss insisted. Tears slid down Sara's check as she laughed and accepted their congratulations.

"Okay, now it's time to get back to work. Leave the young couple alone," Sara's boss escorted the group out of the hall. The rest of the day was wrapped in a glow of wonder. She had thought about marriage, thought that it would happen sometime in the future, just hadn't expected it so soon.

"I wanted this birthday to be one you remembered," Larry had said at the end of the day.

"That I will," Sara responded. "That I will," she repeated to herself after he left.

It had been hard to say goodbye, hard to go back to work the next day. Her head wasn't in her work.

"We've got to tell my parents, and Joy. We have to tell Joy," Sara told him.

"So call them," Larry said. Larry had already told his parents.

"No, I want to see their faces when I tell them. Let's go there this weekend." And so they had arranged to go for Sunday dinner.

She continued to stare at the ring during the ride to her parents.

"I can't wait to tell them. They'll be so happy," Sara said as they pulled into the driveway. "Let's wait till we get inside," she instructed.

"Whatever you say, baby. It's up to you," Larry agreed.

Her parents greeted them at the car door.

"Sara, Larry, so good to see both of you," they said, exchanging hugs and kisses.

"Good to see you, too," Sara said as they walked in the door. As she took off her coat she proceeded to wiggle her finger in front of her mom.

"Sara, is that?" her mom asked.

"Yes, it is, Mom! We're engaged," Sara said with a big smile.

"That's wonderful," Mary said as she hugged her.

"Congratulations, young man," her dad said as he shook Larry's hand.

"You don't look surprised, Dad," Sara said as she hugged her dad. "Larry, did you?"

"I couldn't ask you to marry me without your father's approval, could I?" Larry said.

"You could have, but I think it's sweet that you did," Sara said.

"I knew he was asking, I just didn't know when, though I suspected your birthday may be the day," her dad interjected.

"Mom, you didn't know?"

"I was sworn to secrecy," her dad said, "something hard to do after so many years of marriage."

"I thought something might be up, but I didn't know," Mary said.

"Well, at least I can surprise Joy with the news," Sara said.

With mention of Joy a shadow crossed her parents' faces. "What's the matter, Mom and Dad? Is something wrong?" Sara asked, guessing the worst.

"It seems Joy's cancer has returned," her mom said.

"When? How? How come no one told me?"

"It was just this past week. Joy fell at the dance studio. She didn't want to tell anyone until she knew more, and then you called and said you were coming this weekend so we thought we would wait until now to tell you.”

“So, tell me,” Sara said with a knot welling in her stomach.

“It’s not as bad as it sounds,” her dad said. “She broke her hip but it was a blessing in disguise because it let us know about the cancer. Otherwise it could have spread even farther without anyone knowing.”

“There was no sign of a recurrence?” Sara asked.

“No, none at all, at least none that we are aware of,” her mom chimed in.

“They did a hip replacement, which took away a number of the spots – mets, they are called. There are a few other spots. The doctor says they can be controlled with drugs. Fortunately it hasn’t gone beyond the bones,” her dad continued.

“The doctor says she could live many more years,” her mom added.

“So, she had hip replacement surgery, and no one told me.” Sara was still trying to take all of this in. The diamond that had glowed so brightly just a minute ago now seemed a dull rock.

“We were going to tell you but Joy didn’t want us to. Then when you called about coming home we thought it best to tell you in person.”

She felt guilty for being happy when her sister had been suffering. “I wish I had known. I would have come home.”

“And done what?” her dad asked.

“Take care of the kids, something.”

“The kids are fine. We would have called you if we needed you,” her mom assured her. Instead of being reassured, she felt left out.

“We didn’t want to spoil your week,” her dad added. Sara didn’t know what to say.

“When can I see her?”

“She’s home from the hospital, got home yesterday. They don’t keep anyone in any longer than absolutely necessary. She’s still pretty weak but she’s up and walking. We told her we would come over after dinner.

Her mom’s dinner – chicken, potatoes and gravy, comfort food – stuck in her throat, making it hard to swallow. Her stomach roiled all the way to Joy’s. What would she find there, she wondered?

Would her big sister be her old self, the sister she remembered, or a new self, formed by cancer?

"Maybe we should hold off telling her about the engagement," she said to Larry.

"Why? The news is out. If we don't tell her, someone else will. Don't you want to be the one to break the big news?"

"I know but, it just seems wrong, with all she is going through."

"Don't you think she would want to share in your happiness? It might be nice for her to have some good news."

"I know . . ."

"You are happy, aren't you?"

"Of course, I am. It just seems wrong for me to be so happy when Joy isn't."

"You aren't joined at the hip. There will be times when she will be happy when you aren't," Larry added.

"I guess so," Sara agreed, but not really. She rode in silence the remainder of the drive. She twirled her ring around so that only the band showed, not the diamond, still debating what to say when she got there.

Dale met them at the door as a dog came crashing out followed by Jacob and Ashley.

"Hi, Aunt Sara," they both said, giving her a quick hug before chasing after the dog.

"Lucky," they shouted as they ran.

"Sorry," Dale said as he hugged them. "Good to see you!"

"You've got a dog?" Sara asked.

"You might say he got us. A stray. We are waiting to see if anyone claims him. Come on in," he said, then yelled at the kids, "Stay in the back yard!"

"How are you?" Dale asked as if nothing had happened.

"We're good. How are you?" Sara answered, waiting for the story.

"We are good too," Dale replied.

"Really? But, I thought, I'd heard … Mom said, Joy's cancer," Sara stammered.

"Yeah, but she's doing surprisingly well. Come see for yourself," Dale told them.

Sara exchanged a glance with Larry as they followed Dale into the living room. Joy was propped up in a large reclining chair with flower arrangements and stacks of cards on the coffee table. She smiled as she welcomed Sara and Larry.

"From my students," she remarked, pointing at the cards. "I hope you understand my not getting up," she said as she reached up to hug Sara.

"Of course," Sara said. After Larry hugged Joy, they sat down on the couch.

"How are you?" Sara asked, not sure what else to say, not sure what to expect.

"I'm doing well. Stiff and sore and moving slowly but at least I'm moving."

"But what about . . .?" Sara asked.

"The cancer? It came back but it isn't what I thought it would be."

"What do you mean?"

"I went online and found out there are lots of women just like me, living with mets, living long and full lives."

"Mets?"

"Metastases," Joy responded. "In fact I'm luckier than most. Most of mine were in my hip. This hip replacement should take care of them."

"Besides," Dale chimed in, "we haven't got the results of the biopsy yet. We should know more once we get those. Depending on the results, we should be able to control the spread with drugs. There are a lot of options yet."

"I feel like I was on death row and was given a reprieve," Joy said, tears welling in her eyes. She smiled, "So what's new with you?"

Sara looked over at Larry before turning her diamond back around on her finger and showing Joy.

"We're engaged," she said tentatively.

"That's wonderful," Joy exclaimed. "I'm so happy for you. Come here and give me another hug. This hip may keep me from getting up but I can still give hugs."

"Congratulations," Dale said, shaking Larry's hand. "Not that I'm surprised. We figured this was coming."

"And you'll be my bridesmaid, won't you?" Sara asked Joy.

"Of course," Joy responded.

"And Ashley can be flower girl, and Jacob ring bearer," Sara added.

"Of course. Tell me about it. How did he propose? Have you set a date? We have so much to do."

"I think it's time to check on the kids," Dale said, picking Grace up. "Larry, you want to join me?" he added. Larry quickly jumped up.

"Thanks for getting me out of there," he said as they played with the kids in the back yard.

"Yeah, they were about to go off on wedding plans. Looks like we got out here just in time. Here comes Mary and Tom." He waved to his in-laws from the backyard as they walked up the sidewalk to the side door, Mary carrying two pies.

"I've got dessert," Mary shouted to them.

"We'll be in in a while," Dale shouted back. "Wait till the three of them get going. We are much better off back here," he said to Larry.

"So, are you really doing okay?" Larry asked.

"Today, yes – three days ago, no. It's a roller coaster ride. Right now Joy is recovering and home and in good spirits. The drugs help. We are at the top, you might say. Who knows what tomorrow will bring? The prognosis is not as bad as we had thought at first, so life is good. Where we go next is yet to be determined. But that's true for everyone, isn't it? None of us knows what tomorrow will bring, so let's enjoy today," Dale said as he threw a stick for Lucky to catch. He was reassuring himself as much as Larry.

"That didn't go quite how we had expected," Larry said on the drive home.

"No. I don't know what to think. I need to sort it all out. Joy seems to be okay."

"Are you okay?"

"I've got you, haven't I?"

"That you do."

"I'm okay, really. We'll be okay. And we've got a wedding to plan."

"We've got a life to plan," Larry said, reaching for her hand.

"Tired?" Dale asked as Joy walked, holding on to her walker, exercising her hip after everyone had left.

"Yes, but I'm good," Joy responded. "I'm happy for Sara and Larry. He seems like he's right for Sara. They are both so young, though."

"Younger than we were when we got married, but Larry's pretty level-headed. He's good for her."

"They'll get by. They have their whole life ahead of them."

"As do we," Dale added.

"As do we," Joy said as she winced from pain. "Time to sit down."

Chapter 7

Lucky was quickly becoming a part of the family. Joy had balked at first at the addition.

"What? A dog? What were you thinking?" Dale knew that Joy was starting to feel more like herself when she scolded him once back in her room after the surgery. "The last thing we need is a dog. Who's going to take care of the dog? I can barely manage to take care of myself right now, much less the kids and a dog," she said through the pain.

"Mom will help. Besides, the owner may claim him at any time. He clearly comes from a good home. Someone must be looking for him. I can take him to the pound if you want."

"And make me the bad guy? Haven't our kids been through enough? Their mom in the hospital and their dog in the pound. No way are you taking that dog to the pound." And so it had been settled.

When two weeks had passed with no one claiming Lucky, they thought he was theirs. He had become an established part of their daily routine. He got Dale up at six every morning to let him out. He played with the kids until they got on the bus for school, then settled down for a nap, while Grace climbed over him. Lucky waited at the window, watching for Jacob to get home from kindergarten at noon, and again watching for Ashley's bus.

"Get that dog out of here," Mary would yell each day as he jumped all over the house, greeting first Jacob, then Ashley. "He's going to knock over your mom," she added as Lucky circled around Joy's walker.

Joy's parents and Esther were taking turns helping out, taking Joy to rehab, watching the children and the dog while Dale was at work. This way Joy had round-the-clock help while recovering from surgery. Dale couldn't wait to have their home back to just them, but in the meantime he appreciated the help. Joy filled her days with planning for the Christmas recital. The strains of Christmas carols were comforting to her as she struggled to regain her strength.

"Grandma, there's someone at the door," Joy heard Jacob yell.

"I'll be there in a minute," Mary said while Jacob opened the door. A man stood in the doorway. Lucky ran to the door, barking and jumping on him.

"Whoa there, boy, whoa," he said as he patted Lucky and tried to get him to quiet down.

Mary appeared at the door. "And you are?" she asked.

"Sorry, Lucky hasn't forgotten me though it seems I had forgotten him." The man extended his hand. "I'm Howard Jones. And this here is Lucky," he said, reaching down to pet Lucky after shaking Mary's hand.

"Can I help you?" Mary said, not liking what she was seeing.

"You already have. Seems you've been taking care of my dog for me."

"Why don't you come in, Mr. Jones," Mary said. "Ashley, tell your mom we have company," she instructed as Howard came through the door. He was older, walked hesitantly with a slight limp. What hair he had was silver grey. She brought him into the living room.

"Can I get you something to drink?" Mary asked after introducing him to Joy.

"Call Dale," Joy whispered into her ear.

She called him from the kitchen while getting a glass of iced tea for Mr. Jones. "Dale, we need you here," she said.

"What's wrong, Mom? Is Joy okay?"

"Just get here as fast as you can. There's a man here claiming he's Lucky's owner." Dale put down the phone, reached for his coat and was out the door with a perfunctory nod to his secretary. "Got to get home," he said.

Meanwhile, Howard was regaling Joy and Mary with his life story while Lucky played on the floor with the kids.

"Lucky was my wife's dog actually. Helen loved dogs. Always had to have one or two. She had rescued Lucky from the pound. The runt of the litter, he was ugly even then," Howard said with affection. "The litter had been abandoned in a box along the side of a country road. Someone found them and brought them to the pound. Lucky was the last to be adopted. He truly was a lucky one. If Helen hadn't come along he probably wouldn't be alive today. He had been scheduled to be killed."

"But where have you been for the last two weeks?" Joy asked.

"I've been visiting my sister in Florida. A neighbor was supposed to be taking care of Lucky. Apparently he got away. I didn't get home till yesterday but when I called the pound they gave me your number. I looked up your address and thought I would see for myself. I'm sorry about just showing up on your doorstep."

"What about your wife, Helen?" Joy asked.

Tears welled up as he struggled to answer her question.

"She's gone, died over two months ago. Now Lucky's all I have left of her."

Joy and Mary exchanged glances. They knew what they had to do, but how to tell the kids?

"We are so sorry for your loss, Mr. Jones," Mary said.

"Call me Howard. It's okay. She had been sick for a long time. Lucky stayed by her side throughout the illness. Alzheimer's. She had already been diagnosed when we got Lucky from the pound. We thought he might be a comfort to her and he was. He seemed to understand. When she didn't remember anyone else, she seemed to know Lucky. He had a way of soothing her when she became distraught."

"That must have been very hard for you," Joy said.

"Yes, well, she's no longer suffering. In many ways I had lost her, lost the woman I had married, years before her physical death."

Dale entered the room, trying to quickly take in what was transpiring.

"Howard, this is my husband, Dale. Lucky is Howard's dog," Joy introduced Dale.

"He was my wife's dog," Howard clarified. "I think I have taken up enough time from you good people. Lucky and I better be on our way." Howard stood up and called to Lucky, "Lucky, come." Lucky came to him, wagging his tale. Howard snapped a leash on him.

Ashley and Jacob stood up and looked over at Lucky, not understanding what was happening.

"Here Lucky," Jacob called. Lucky whined but stayed by Howard's side.

"Why are you taking our dog?" Ashley asked.

"Honey," Joy intervened, "it's not our dog. Lucky belongs to Mr. Jones. Remember we told you he belonged to someone else."

"But that was before, now he belongs to us," Jacob cried. "Don't you, Lucky? You belong here with us." Lucky started to pull on his leash.

"Lucky, stay," Howard ordered. "I'm awfully sorry, but I can't lose Lucky, too. You understand, don't you?" He appealed to Joy.

"Yes, we do. Jacob, Ashley, Lucky is Mr. Jones' dog. Say goodbye," Joy told them. They both went over and gave Lucky hugs.

"Don't forget us," Jacob whispered into Lucky's ear. Lucky just wagged his tail. Dale walked with Howard to his car, the kids watching from the window the same way Lucky had looked out the window each day, watching for their bus.

"I'm sorry about this," Howard repeated. "Your wife, is she ill?"

"Breast cancer, but she's in recovery."

"I'm sorry."

"No need to be sorry. Lucky is your dog. The kids will just have to accept that." Howard put Lucky in the back seat of the car, said goodbye to Dale and drove away. Dale turned to face the house, seeing the faces of his two oldest children still in the window. He took a deep breath and returned inside.

"Come on, Jacob," Ashley said as Dale entered the living room. She gave him a look that expressed her feelings of betrayal before leading her brother out of the room. "Let's go."

"That didn't go well," Dale said.

"I know, but what else could we do?"

"We can't get another dog, not with you being laid up."

"I know, honey. They'll get over it," Joy assured him.

But will I, Dale asked himself. After cold shoulders during dinner and bedtime, despite himself Dale found himself saying, "When Mommy gets better, maybe we can get another dog."

"I don't want another dog. I just want Lucky. I miss Lucky," Ashley whined.

"But Mr. Jones needs Lucky too. He is his dog."

"I need him more," Ashley insisted.

"Maybe we can visit Lucky this weekend."

"Can we, Daddy?"

"I'll see what we can work out," he told her.

He cursed himself the next day as he searched the Internet for a Howard Jones. "There are a hundred Jones in the phone book. Four H Jones, not a single Howard. How will I find him?" he muttered to himself. "Why didn't I get his phone number yesterday?"

He gave the job to his secretary who finally came up with a Howard Jones on the other side of town from where Dale lived.

"Thank you, I'll call tonight and see if he's the right H. Jones." He found it hard to believe Lucky could have travelled so far to his house but was willing to give it a try.

He didn't have to. He pulled into his driveway the same time as Howard.

"Mr. Jones. Good to see you. I was going to call you."

"And I was going to call you. Seems Lucky got loose again. I thought possibly he might have come here."

"Let's find out." Dale let himself and Howard in. Joy's mom was finishing getting dinner ready.

"Mary, Lucky is missing again. Do you know anything about it?"

"No, haven't seen him."

"Where are the kids?"

"They've been playing quietly upstairs since Ashley got home from school. Can I get you anything, Mr. Jones?"

"Howard," Howard insisted. "I'm fine. Sure smells good in here, though," Dale took Howard into the living room to visit with Joy while he checked on the kids.

"Ashley, Jacob, come here." They ran down the stairs.

"Mr. Jones says Lucky is missing again. Have you seen him?"

"No, Dad," they both said.

"Are you sure?" Something didn't seem right.

"Yes."

"Okay. What are you doing?"

"Just playing, Daddy." He excused them and they ran back upstairs. He quietly followed them up the stairs, opened the door to their room and there was Lucky.

"Ashley, Jacob," he began.

"But Dad, he found us. He was out back when I came home," Ashley said.

"That's no excuse for lying. Mr. Jones is waiting in the living room. We have to bring Lucky downstairs."

The kids walked reluctantly downstairs, dragging their heels. Lucky seemed happy to see Howard but when he got up to leave, he slunk over to Ashley.

"Sorry, boy. We've got to go," he said while dragging Lucky out the door.

"I'm sorry about this," Howard told Dale.

"I'm sorry, too. The kids are taking this quite hard. Do you think we could visit Lucky on the weekend?"

"I don't see why not. I'm too old to keep up with Lucky. It would do him good to have some kids to play with." Dale arranged for the play date.

Inside the kids were pouting. "I talked to Mr. Jones. We can go see Lucky on the weekend. Okay?" he lifted both kids onto his lap. "I know it's not the same as having him live with us, but at least you get to see him, and maybe he can stay with us sometimes." Ashley and Jacob were slightly cheered by the promise of a visit.

When Dale came home the next day he saw the becoming-familiar car in the driveway again.

"Howard, did Lucky run away again?" Dale asked when he came into the living room.

"No, but it seems Lucky just isn't happy with me. And the truth of the matter is, I've been thinking about spending the winter in Florida, at my sister's. The senior apartment complex where she lives doesn't allow dogs. The only reason I haven't gone yet was because of Lucky," he said, looking over to where Lucky was sitting with Ashley. "But it seems Lucky has found himself another home, a home where he is needed more than I need him. So now I can go. That is – if you'll have him."

Dale looked at the kids and Joy with a big smile. "Of course we'll have him. Right, kids?" The kids just smiled and hugged Lucky.

"And you're welcome to visit him any time. Would you like to stay for dinner?" Joy asked.

"Don't mind if I do. It smells great. Thank you."

Ashley and Jacob went running out of the house, laughing, Lucky in tow.

"It seems we have a dog," Dale commented as he helped Joy into the dining room later for dinner.

"And a new friend," Joy added, looking over at Howard who was telling stories to the kids.

"One can never have too many friends," Dale said.

Chapter 8

Kathleen's head felt like it was going to explode, her stomach rolled. She looked up and thought, "Where am I?" Then, even more important she asked herself, "where is the bathroom?"

"Good morning, sleepy head," a male voice said.

Oh, no, she thought, what had she done?

"What time is it?" she mumbled. She vaguely remembered the man as an acquaintance from the bar. They had been playing pool. He had been good, very good. One of the few players that posed a challenge to her ascendance. She had continued to drink and play pool long past her usual leaving time. What had she been thinking, she wondered again.

"Did we?"

"No, sweetie, you passed out before I got you here. Believe me, if we were to do it, you would remember," he said. "You don't have to look so relieved. Here," he handed her a mug of coffee. Kathleen wasn't sure she could keep it down.

"What time is it?" she asked again.

"Around seven thirty."

"Shit. I have to get home," she said, making a beeline for the bathroom where she relieved herself, slapped some water on her face and ran a comb through her hair.

"Here, baby, this will help," the man offered her a snort of cocaine. "It will pick you up."

"No," Kathleen said, pushing past him to the door.

"Your loss," he said as he took the cocaine himself.

"Where's my car?" Kathleen panicked.

"At the Green Door. You were in no shape to drive last night." He drove her to the bar where she jumped out without a goodbye in her haste to get home. She was in trouble.

What had she done, Kathleen kept asking herself as she drove home, frantic to get there in time for her grandfather to make his eight o'clock breakfast. She got to use her grandfather's car as long as she kept gas in it and he had it every morning for his coffee klatch with friends. It had never been a problem until today.

She pulled into the driveway. Her grandfather was waiting for her. How could she face him, she asked herself. But face him she must. She handed him the keys without saying a word.

"You're late," he commented. She didn't respond. She walked past her mom and hurried down stairs to her room. Maybe she could stay there forever or at least until her stomach stopped shifting gears, she thought.

Esther and Erick looked at each other. The words remained unsaid as Erick went to meet his friends, leaving Esther sitting at the kitchen table, still in her bathrobe, drinking coffee.

"What was I thinking," Kathleen kept asking herself. A slippery slope. Stay away from slippery people and slippery places. She remembered this from the Narcotics Anonymous meetings she had been required to attend as part of her probation years ago. What a waste, she had thought at the time. She had not been an addict. Yes, she used drugs, but in a controlled way. She had never crossed the line to addiction, or so she had told herself. She had been the one selling the drugs. She wasn't about to cut into her profits by using to excess. Besides, she needed her wits about her to succeed in a position usually held by men. She was more interested in the money and what it could buy than the drugs. The court ordered NA meetings had given her access to a whole new group of buyers as she attended the "meeting after the meeting," hooking up with attendees of both the NA and AA meeting, usually at a local bar.

That had been before her last prison sentence, back when the courts had still thought she could be rehabilitated. Back before they realized she was the dealer, not the user. They couldn't quite believe that this innocent looking young woman was dealing drugs. She put on a good show for the court. It was part of what made her so valuable to the network. She had her sights on moving up the ranks in her chosen profession. No, she wasn't a user, nor had she gone the route of prostitute. She could see that the real money lay in being the one who called the shots, ran the show. She was too smart to let some pimp get most of her hard-earned money, she had told herself.

Still, something must have sunk in from those meetings. She remembered about slippery slopes. Slippery people. She didn't know who this guy was, but she knew he was a slippery person. Hanging out at the Green Door was a slippery place. She knew that and yet she had continued to go there. Why, she didn't know. Maybe out of boredom. She had put that life behind her, didn't want to go back and yet, there she was. The drugs had found her. She didn't want to go down that path again.

She slept through her morning class, only getting up after noon. She showered and tried to get herself back to normal. She was contemplating going back to bed when her mother called down to her.

"Kathleen, the school just called. Seems there's some kind of trouble with Scott. I've got class. You'll have to take care of it," Esther said. No asking if she would do it, just telling her. Mom must figure she didn't deserve a break. Kathleen had lost custody of her sons when she was sentenced to prison years ago. Since getting out she was trying to forge a relationship with them as part of her new life. Esther was the legal guardian of the boys which is why she had been called, not Kathleen.

"Okay, Mom," Kathleen responded. She got the car keys back from her grandpa and headed to the high school.

Kathleen wasn't sure what to do. This was her first time being called to school for either of her sons. Not that she was unfamiliar with the vice principal's office. She was all too familiar from her years of high school. Still it was a different vice principal, different secretary. Hopefully no one remembered her. Josh and Scott had never given their grandma a reason to pick them up at the vice principal's office, until today.

Pastor Joe had known it was too good to be true. Almost a month and no phone calls. He wanted to believe it, wanted to believe the change of schools had been what Stephanie had needed to straighten out her life. She complained at first, but then had been strangely compliant, almost seeming to be happy about the change. He knew she had been happy to be rid of the school uniform. He had been worried. It had almost seemed like rewarding her for bad behavior, buying clothes for school, but without a uniform, Stephanie did need more school clothes. Maybe she had just needed to get away from the label PK – preacher's kid. Everyone at St. Luke's knew she was the pastor's daughter, with all the expectations that came with that title. Now his hopes had been dashed by one of those dreaded phone calls. Almost a month and no calls to the vice principal's office. He knew it was too good to be true, yet he had hoped.

Stephanie was sitting with a boy he didn't know. Must be a classmate, he thought. Now what?

A woman was already in the vice principal's office. He thought she looked vaguely familiar but wasn't sure where he knew her from.

"Good, Pastor, we were just getting started. As I was telling Ms. Reese here," Reese, Joe's brain clicked, maybe related to Dale? "It seems your children have gotten themselves into some trouble in the cafeteria. Seems there was a fight."

"Whatever it was, I'm sure my Scott had nothing to do with it," Kathleen protested.

"That's not what the lunchroom supervisor told me."

"Well, she's wrong," Kathleen insisted.

"What exactly happened?" Joe asked.

"Your daughter knocked a tray out of a student's hands," he said to Joe then turned to Kathleen, "And your son punched him."

"Then he must have had it coming to him," Kathleen said.

"Did they tell you what provoked them?" Joe asked.

"They claim the boy had taken food from another student, but the lunch supervisor didn't see anything."

"Well, if that's what my son said, I'm sure that's what happened," Kathleen said.

"Ms. Reese, you aren't Scott's legal guardian, are you?" he said as he looked through a file on his desk.

"No, his grandmother is. She couldn't make it. But I'm still his mother."

"I see," he said, making a note.

"Just what do you see?" Kathleen asked, ready to take him on. She felt the hair rising on her neck. This was too reminiscent of her years in high school.

"Nothing," he said.

"If it's nothing then why did you bring it up?" Kathleen wasn't ready to drop it.

"And it seems Stephanie has a bit of a record from her previous school," he added, looking through Stephanie's file from St. Luke's.

"Could we talk to the kids," Joe changed the subject.

The vice principal called his secretary over the intercom and told her to send Stephanie and Scott in.

"What do you have to say for yourself?" Joe asked Stephanie.

"Warren Taylor, he was picking on the special needs kids. Took food off of some of the kids' trays. That's why I took his tray."

"And he was going to hit Stephanie. That's why I hit him," Scott said.

"Did the lunchroom supervisor see it happening?" Joe continued.

"No, she was in another area of the lunch room. Besides, she's Warren's buddy. She always overlooks what he does."

"And why did you get involved in this?" Kathleen asked Scott.

"What she said. He's just plain mean. Someone has to show him he can't treat people like that," Scott said.

"See," Kathleen said, "they were provoked."

"That still didn't justify what they did. No need to discuss this further," the vice principal replied. Then, turning to Scott and Stephanie, he added, "You both get detention. You'll be eating lunch in detention and spending the afternoon after school in detention for one week. That should give you plenty of time to think about what you did." Then he dismissed all four of them.

"Well, that didn't go well," Joe commented as they walked down the hall, trying to make small talk.

"You just keep your daughter away from my son," Kathleen snapped.

"So your son is innocent."

"He was just following your daughter's lead. Scott's never been in trouble before this. Your daughter's the one with the record. Keep her away from him."

"With pleasure," Joe muttered under his breath. He hoped he never had to deal with her again. She couldn't possibly be related to the Reeses he knew, who attended his church.

"So it begins again," he said to his daughter as they drove home. Stephanie had been waiting for him to break the silence.

"You always taught me to stand up for those less fortunate. Warren is a bully."

"And so you have undertaken to singlehandedly put him in his place?"

"Well, somebody has to."

"But why does it have to be you? You've hardly been there long enough to know anyone, much less know who the 'bad guys' are."

"Dad, I know a bully when I see one. I would think you would be proud of me."

"Well, we'll see. And stay away from that Reese boy."

"I didn't ask him to take on Warren. He did that on his own."

"I don't care, stay away from him anyway."

"Sure, Dad," Stephanie said as she slouched down in her seat.

"I just don't want you to get off to the wrong start in this school. I want things to be different."

"They are different, Dad, you just don't see it."

"Then show me," Joe said. Stephanie remained silent the rest of the way home.

It was different, but she didn't know how to convince her dad. She felt so much less pressure here than in the church school where it seemed everyone's eyes were upon her. It was bad enough that she had to live in a fish bowl with all those prying eyes. She didn't want to attend school in a fish bowl as well. She wanted to sink into the walls of the hallway, blend into the lockers where everyone would leave her alone. She hadn't intended to draw attention to herself, but some things you just couldn't let slide.

Her mind went back to the episode, when she had confronted Warren.

"Give them back their food."

"Who's going to make me?"

"I will if no one else will," that was when she had grabbed hold of Warren's tray and its contents spilled on the floor. She would have dumped the tray on his head if Scott hadn't intervened, hitting Warren before he could hit Stephanie.

"I don't need your help," she told him.

"Well, I accept your thanks anyway."

"Who said thanks?" Just then they had been grabbed by Mrs. Johnson, the lunchroom supervisor.

"She dumped my food and when I went to pick it up he hit me," Warren whined.

"He took the food from Ralph and Steven," Stephanie pointed to their table.

"No, I didn't. They just decided to pick on me," Warren whined some more. "I wouldn't take anything from Ralph or Steven, right guys?"

Ralph looked over at Warren then ducked his head back down, not saying anything. Steven didn't look up, out of fear of Warren.

"There, you see," Warren insisted.

"All right you two. You're going to the vice principal's office." When they protested she replied, "You can tell it to the vice principal."

Stephanie hadn't wanted to get in trouble. She was liking it here. She was able to take advance placement math and science classes, something not offered at St. Luke's. She didn't want to jeopardize her chances to continue in these classes. Not everyone was allowed in them. Still she couldn't just sit quiet in the face of injustice. Her dad had taught her as much.

Scott was in her home room, English lit and social science classes. He wasn't the smartest in class, was not taking the college prep courses she was enrolled in, but was taking shop. She hadn't noticed him, but apparently he had noticed her.

Scott had always had an affinity for the underdog. He befriended those without a friend, was a friend to all. Coming into a new school a month after school started, he figured she was the odd man out, or the odd woman out. He thought she could use a friend. He also recognized her from his grandma's church. He didn't always go with her, preferring to stay home on Sunday mornings with his great granddad and brother, still he went on special days, like Christmas and Easter and other occasions.

Esther didn't force the boys to go to church with her. She saw how little good it had done for Kathleen. She had signed them up for Sunday school when they were younger, but once they hit sixth grade both boys had opted out. Esther hoped the early instructions would be enough to give them a base for growth when they were ready, but she didn't push it. She had considered going back to her old church, the one with the large youth group, but since the boys showed little interest in that, she decided to stay with her current church where she felt comfortable and where her son and other grandchildren attended. All she asked was that Josh and Scott go with her on holidays like Christmas, Easter and Mother's Day.

Scott had seen just enough of Stephanie those times to be intrigued. She didn't look happy, didn't look like she felt comfortable in church, or even in her own skin. She seemed a little lost, angry and lost. That intrigued him. He had not found the right words to start a conversation with her until that day.

"You stay away from that girl," Kathleen instructed him on the way home.

"Why? She was just standing up to Warren. Someone should have stood up to him before this," Scott asserted.

"I don't care. She's trouble. I know her type. Better stay away from her."

"How do you know that?" Scott challenged her.

"I just do," Kathleen insisted, ending the discussion as far as she was concerned. She reminds me of me, Kathleen thought to herself. She didn't want to tell Scott that. They already knew too much about my past, she thought. They don't need to know more, she told herself as she drove Scott home.

She reminds me of me, Kathleen repeated to herself. "I don't like her. She's trouble," Kathleen added for Scott's benefit to reinforce what she had already said. She also didn't like herself too much just then.

Chapter 9

Joy was happy to be back at the dance studio. She had been determined that she would be one of the ones who recovered in four weeks rather than six months. She still wasn't cleared for driving and couldn't do everything she used to, not yet anyway, but she was walking and hardly needed her walker any more.

"Take it, just in case," Esther had prodded before driving her to the studio, putting Grace in her car seat then helping Joy get in.

"All right," Joy agreed, "but you'll see I don't need it."

She wasn't ready to take over her classes again. It just felt good being there, seeing what progress had been made and sitting in on classes, making suggestions here and there. She had appreciated all of the homemade cards from her students, the flowers her instructors had sent and their visits to see how she was doing and keep her informed, but now it was time to see for herself how everything was going rather than rely on second hand information.

It had been especially good to get back to her breast cancer rehab class. This one she was able to teach since it primarily required upper body exercises for arms and chest. There were some that were done standing but she could work around these.

The group had visited her at her home as soon as they heard she was up for visitors. They had brought over cupcakes and hot chocolate from Joy's favorite bakery.

"This is so good," Joy exclaimed as she bit into a chocolate crème-filled cupcake. "Heavenly. Thank you so much." They proceeded to fill her in on how class was going. Since the exercises were routine, they had been continuing on their own without a leader, each taking a turn and helping out as needed.

"It will be good to have you back with us," Janet said, stating what all were thinking.

"Yes, it's just not the same without you." Even though the group had been together less than a year, they had already developed close bonds due to their shared struggle with breast cancer. Six to ten women regularly attended each week, depending on their schedules. They knew about each other's diagnosis, husbands, children, pets and struggles.

"When do you think you'll be rejoining us," Audrey asked.

"Yesterday wouldn't be too soon," Joy said with a smile. "Soon. Maybe in a week or two. It doesn't require two good legs to do arm-strengthening exercises. By the way, how is Susan doing?"

The group looked at each other awkwardly. "She had a relapse, too, only it appears hers has spread to her lungs and brain. The prognosis isn't good." Finally Sharon filled her in.

Joy didn't know what to say. They had already had a number of women come and go. Some stayed long enough to regain their strength then stopped attending; others had had relapses and dropped out while undergoing more chemo and radiation. Some, though, kept coming back each week as much for the emotional support as the physical support.

"But she'll beat it," Audrey added. "She's a fighter. Just like you." There was another awkward pause before Audrey added, "Did you know Joan's husband is taking her on a second honeymoon to Paris," changing the subject as she pointed to another group member. The conversation then shifted to travel and dreams of travel.

The group met twice a week for one hour but members usually stayed longer than that, talking, sharing stories and laughing so that Joy had started providing tea and coffee for them. Others brought snacks or desserts till the time extended to two hours. Joy tried to keep track of each member's progress, recording information in a notebook and posting news on her website blog. She had stopped blogging at first while recovering from the surgery, but as her strength returned she needed more to do than read and watch TV, so she had started again, filling readers in on her latest setback and prognosis. Her blog had become an additional forum for support, not just for her, but for others as well. Joy was learning so much from these women and other women on-line. She was learning what it is to live with "mets," that it's not the end of the world, nor the end of her life. With any luck she could live to a ripe old age and die from something completely unrelated. All of this gave her hope as she worked out her treatment plans with her doctor.

The biopsy had confirmed what they had expected, cancer. Now that she was stronger her doctor was trying out different medications.

"We'll be closely monitoring the mets that remain, checking your blood regularly for recurrences. If the first drug doesn't work, there are others to try. Each woman is different and cancers are different as well. What works for one woman, won't work for another. And sometimes one drug works for awhile and then stops being effective. That's why we want to monitor this closely."

Joy hung onto the hope that the worst was over; that she had many good years ahead of her as she continued to get used to her new hip. "Good as new," she told her friends, "In fact, better because it is new. I'm the bionic woman," she joked.

She enjoyed the warm welcomes reverberating throughout the hallway as she walked through the building, barely holding on to her walker. When all the welcomes were over and everyone was busy in class, Joy found herself drawn to the room that had been set aside as a studio for her sister, Sara. She gazed at the painting on the wall outside. This time it was a happy reminder of where she had been, what she had come through and her progress. She paused and thought of the small child that had once existed in that distended belly.

"Doctor," she had asked hesitantly at her last appointment, "do you think, I mean if I had treated the first occurrence more aggressively? ..." She couldn't bring herself to say the words, but she knew both the doctor and Dale knew what she was referring to. If she had terminated her pregnancy and pursued a more aggressive treatment, would she have been less likely to have a recurrence? She felt disloyal to her child for even suggesting it, felt like a terrible mother for even thinking it, much less mentioning it. Still she had to know. Not that she would have done it any differently, she just needed to know.

"We don't know. No one can say. Maybe, but maybe not. You may have done everything possible and still had a recurrence. This is not an exact science. This is the human body. For all we know, there is so much that remains a mystery."

The doctor's words came back to her as she viewed the picture. She was so grateful for her little Grace, she thought as she paused, then proceeded to go watch the dance classes.

Chapter 10

"What's up little brother? You look worried," Kathleen asked Dale.

"Nothing," Dale said.

"Don't lie to me. I can see the creases in your forehead. What's wrong?" Kathleen insisted. She had come over on her night off from Pizza Hut to work on the web-site she had designed for Dale's business last year.

"It's nothing, just all this paperwork related to Joy's surgery and treatment. It's been over a month and I'm just getting some of them. Just when I think I'm done paying for it, another bill comes through. Even with insurance, it's so expensive. Don't know what we would do without insurance." Dale shuffled the stack of papers. "There's the doctor's bill, the surgeon's bill, the anesthesiologist, not to mention the hospital and ambulance. Everyone who pokes their nose into the room for a minute charges, even when all they do is look at her chart and leave. And the itemized items."

"Does Joy know about this?"

"No, I instructed the hospital to send all bills here to my business rather than home. She has enough to deal with without worrying about this. I don't want to upset her."

"But she has a right to know."

"No, it will just upset her. She worries about money as it is. She would just worry more. Besides, what can we do?"

"Not knowing might cause her more concern. Maybe she could help you with the paperwork."

"Trust me, it's better this way."

"If you say so. Maybe I can help with the paperwork," Kathleen offered.

"No, not right now anyway. Thanks for the offer. For now I've got it covered."

Kathleen respected his wishes even though she thought him in the wrong. She had become close to Joy throughout the past year. So much so that when she found herself slipping back into the hole that had been her past life, Joy was the person she had confided in, much to the surprise of both of them.

She hadn't planned on saying anything, didn't want to bother Joy with her problems when she had her own problems to deal with, but Joy had a knack for knowing when she was holding something back.

"What's going on with you?" Joy had insisted one afternoon before dance lessons began. Kathleen had put together a web-site for Joy as well and helped maintain it. She had come over to work on the web-site and help out with Grace while Esther went to class.

"Something's wrong, I can tell." Joy wouldn't let it go.

Finally Kathleen admitted, "I feel like I'm sinking into a deep hole but I can't seem to stop it."

"What are you doing?"

"Not much, maybe that's the problem. Maybe I need to be doing more but I don't know what. Something more than what I am doing."

"No one expects you to remain at Pizza Hut forever. It's just a temporary way station on your journey."

"It's so boring," Kathleen complained. "I've started going out at night after work," she confessed.

"I know. Esther has been worried."

"And then one night I ended up at this man's apartment. Someone I barely knew. He offered me drugs. It would have been so easy to take them," Kathleen paused. Joy waited for her to be ready to talk again.

"But you didn't take them," Joy said tentatively.

"No, but I wanted to, just for the moment. I wanted to forget everything."

"But you didn't."

"I didn't but I could have. It would have been so easy. What was I thinking?"

"Perhaps you weren't thinking."

"That's precisely the problem. I need more in my life. My classes are okay but work is boring. I need more but I don't know what. I'm afraid of falling into that hole again and never making it out."

"You do need more in your life. Sounds to me like you need to find your passion. It was easy for me. I always knew what I wanted to do. Dancing was and is my passion. I realize how lucky I am. Not everyone has that clarity. They struggle to find the one thing that gives their life meaning. What is your passion?"

"I have no idea. Right now I would just be happy to stay out of that hole."

"But you need more. When you find that, it will help keep you out of that hole. Only you can find it. No one can find it for you."

"I wish I knew what it was."

"I'll pray for you," Joy offered. Kathleen was not a religious person, did not attend church. She usually resented any such offers of prayers as pious crap, but with Joy it was different. Joy didn't preach. Kathleen was actually grateful for her prayer. Maybe it would help. At least it wouldn't hurt.

"Thank you," she told Joy. "Maybe I do need prayer."

Chapter 11

Joy loved her mother and mother-in-law but she was beginning to feel claustrophobic from all of the attention and her lack of space. She had come to treasure her mornings home alone with Grace while Jacob and Ashley were at school. She would sit quietly with her coffee while Grace played. She also missed her dance warm-ups. It had been a quiet time to meditate and commune with God.

At fifteen months, Grace had finally started to understand the meaning of "No!" She was crawling and pulling herself up to take tentative steps, but she played safely in her play area, the room they had baby-proofed and set off from the rest of the house with a baby gate. Sometimes she played quietly for as long as twenty minutes. Twenty minutes of quiet! What a treasure for Joy.

Now she didn't have to watch Grace because someone was always here, watching Grace and Joy. That was the problem. She felt like she was living under a microscope with everyone watching her every step lest she fall again. It was stifling. She didn't even have dance any more. As soon as she was able, she started walking outside, first on the sidewalk, using her walker. As she grew stronger and became more adventurous, she started venturing out on the uneven ground of the yard. Her current sitter would watch her from the window. Joy knew she was being watched but at least she was outside and moving.

When she first went out, Lucky had whined to go with her.

"No, boy. I'm too unsteady to hold your leash just yet." As he continued to whine the whole time she was outside, Joy finally relented, allowing him to walk alongside and about the yard as she walked. He seemed to know instinctively not to jump up on her. He would stray but never too far so she was able to forego the leash. Where he would jump and play with the kids, he was quieter with her. He must have learned from his years with Helen and her Alzheimer's. Joy grew to love their time together. Lucky didn't infringe on her space in the same way that human companions did. She felt free to pursue her own thoughts.

As she grew stronger yet, she started walking in the wooded area behind their home. Dale had bought five acres along with their house with the thought of having the extra space for hunting. He didn't have much time to pursue this passion because of the requirements of running a business and raising a family; still, he kept sacred the hunter's holiday, November 15, the beginning of hunting season. Even if he didn't catch a buck, he loved being out in the woods. He also tried his hand at bow-hunting in October with what free time he could find. It wasn't much, especially this year since Joy needed him at home. He wasn't sure he would be hunting this year.

As Joy began to explore further and further in to the woods, she was starting to understand why Dale loved hunting. While their property was posted "No Hunting," she made sure to wear a bright orange jacket when she ventured into the woods.

"We need an orange jacket for you, boy," she told Lucky. "You look way too much like a deer." She had tried keeping Lucky at home, tying him up in the backyard when she went into the woods but he had whined and barked so much that she couldn't find the peace she was seeking, so she gave in and let him join her.

"Remind me to talk to Dale about getting you a jacket," she said to him as she let him off his leash.

In the woods she was finally free to face all those thoughts she had been hiding from. It had been a roller coaster ride at first from shock, anger and denial at the initial diagnosis, to relief and even joy when her doctor explained the prognosis wasn't as bad as she had feared. Now she was learning to live with her chronic condition. She had good days and bad days. In the woods she was free to contemplate all that she refused to allow to surface at home. At home she tried to remain strong for the sake of Dale and the kids. Here she could be vulnerable, could cry, could contemplate all outcomes, even the most feared.

"What's the worst that could happen?" she asked herself.

"I could die."

"Is death the worst? Everybody dies."

"But not willingly."

"Remember, I have conquered death. You have nothing to fear," or so she tried to tell herself in her imaginary dialogue with God. There are worse things than death, she told herself, but right now she couldn't think of them. She had plenty of fears. She feared leaving her children without a mother. She so wanted to watch them grow to adulthood, help them along their paths. She wanted to grow old with Dale. Dale was forever, till death do . . . She couldn't go any further. Kids grow up and move out, leave you. Marriage was for a lifetime.

Then, after contemplating the worst, she was able to put it behind her and go home ready to smile again, put on a good face for those around her.

When she was feeling her lowest, Lucky would come over and nuzzle her as if to bring her back to reality and let her know she was loved. She would rub his back, look at the leaves falling from the trees and remember she was still alive, still had so much to live for.

She was able to share some of this on her blog. Two weeks after her surgery she was back at it.

I'm sorry I haven't been blogging for a while. I've had a setback. My cancer is back, requiring emergency surgery on my hip. The good news is most of the mets, metastases, were located in my hip so they were removed. I'll be starting a new drug routine to keep the remainder from growing, also drugs for my bones. So now I have to adjust to another new reality, from breast cancer survivor to having a chronic condition. The treatment is different, not as aggressive. They don't want to bring in the 'big guns' just yet. The idea is to manage this over the long term, not cure it. I don't know what it is to have a chronic condition, but I know there are many people who manage to live long full lives with chronic conditions – MS, Lou Gehrig's disease, Parkinson's, Alzheimer's, to name a few. If they can manage, so can I.

The prognosis isn't as bad as I first thought. This disease will get me eventually but not today, not this week or this month, maybe not for ten years or more. In the meantime I plan to live each day as fully as possible.

Hundreds of comments of support followed her announcement from people who knew her from the dance studio, former students, parents of students, church members, as well as other cancer survivors offering their own words of support. Joy was overwhelmed by the outpouring, not sure whether to cry. Now she felt a responsibility to all of these people, to keep them informed, to live for them as well.

The first Sunday she made it to church after the surgery she had been surrounded by well-wishers.

"We've been praying for you," they all told her. Pastor Joe welcomed her back from the pulpit and included her in the communal prayers. It had all been overwhelming. She appreciated the prayers, but the attention was too much at times. It was a relief to find her quiet space in the woods, away from prying eyes and well-wishers. Sometimes there can be too much of a good thing.

Chapter 12

"Daddy, what about my First Communion?" Ashley asked while brushing her teeth. Since Joy's broken hip, Dale had taken over responsibility for getting the kids ready for bed each night. It was hard for Joy to climb up and down the stairs multiple times. She came down for breakfast in the morning then spent the day downstairs and only went back upstairs when ready for bed.

"What?" Dale asked.

"My First Communion." Ashley repeated. Dale paused. These were the things Joy usually took care of. Ordinarily he would have told Ashley to talk to her mom. But then ordinarily Ashley would have gone to Joy, not him. These weren't ordinary times. "Did you forget, Daddy?"

"No, of course not," Dale lied. "I'll talk to your mom about it." Dale doubted Ashley had been fooled but at least she didn't say anything more about it.

"What did you want?" Dale asked as he tucked her into bed. He didn't know about First Communion. It hadn't been a big deal for him. When he had first joined New Beginnings as a teenager, he had been baptized and invited to the table of communion. No fuss had been made about "First" communion. He suspected the same had been true for Joy. Since joining the Lutheran church, he realized things were different. He was learning to appreciate the ritual, still, the idea that First Communion was a big deal was new to him. He hadn't given it much thought. He had other thoughts on his mind. But apparently Ashley had been giving it some thought.

"Katy's parents are taking her out to dinner."

"Is that what you want?"

"No, I think I'd rather have pizza."

"I think that could be arranged. I'll talk to your mother about it."

He went back downstairs to rejoin Joy in the living room.

"Ashley was asking about First Communion," he told her.

"When is it?" Joy was taken aback by the statement. Where had this come from? How had she missed this?

"Next Sunday."

"How could I have missed this? I should know about these things."

"Honey, you've had plenty on your mind.

"Nothing more important than my little girl. Cancer is no excuse. What do they do for First Communion in the Lutheran church?"

"I don't know, but Ashley wants pizza."

"Should we invite my parents?"

"I guess it wouldn't hurt. My mom will be there. I don't think we have to make a big deal out of it, do we? Maybe we should postpone it till you are back on your feet."

"I think it's a little late for that. I don't want Ashley missing out because of me. I'll talk to Ashley about it tomorrow." Inwardly, Joy chided herself. How could she have forgotten about this? She had never missed important events in her children's life.

"Does she need a new dress?" she asked. Joy remembered other First Communions since they had joined St. Luke's. The children didn't get dressed up, but they still wore good clothes.

"I think she can just wear one she already has." Joy was surprised at this role reversal. She didn't think she liked it. It used to be her telling Dale where the kids were concerned. Why hadn't Ashley come to her?

Joy and Dale sat together as Ashley received her first communion, watching her accept the wafer of bread in her hands with an "Amen" and smiling at them as she returned. They didn't know whether she was happier about Communion or the pizza afterwards. Joy teared up as she watched her daughter. A life milestone, she thought. Like getting her period, her first date, graduation, marriage. Would she be around for them? Dale leaned over and whispered, as if knowing what she was thinking.

"There will be many more such occasions," he reassured her.

Chapter 13

Joy insisted on holding Thanksgiving at her home again. Her mom and mother-in-law both tried to talk her out of it, insisting it would be too much for her.

"Let her go," Dale had told them both. "Her mind is made up. You know how Joy gets once her mind is made up." And well they did.

"But you can help me," Joy told them. "I won't turn down help."

With their help, Thanksgiving went smoothly. It had been exhausting for Joy, more so than she had expected. She was barely up for the celebratory glass of sparkling wine with Sara and Esther as they had done the year before.

After one sip she had excused herself, "Sorry, time for me to go to bed. Maybe next year," she told them. This year Kathleen had been included in the group. They finished off the bottle then headed for their respective homes.

Sara had been worried about Joy doing Thanksgiving. She felt guilty about her inability to help out since her move to Detroit.

"Don't worry, we'll put you to work on the day of Thanksgiving," Joy had assured her. "There's always plenty to do." And that there was. She and Larry had finally kicked Joy out of the kitchen while they did dishes, ably assisted by Kathleen, Esther and Mary.

"Joy looked tired. I hope she didn't overdo it today," Sara said to her mom that night.

"Of course, anyone would be tired after hosting Thanksgiving for that brood."

Sara replied, "I know, but don't you think she looked more tired than usual?"

"She's fine, Sara," her mom assured her. Sara tried to feel reassured.

Her Christmas gift to Joy was tickets to the Nutcracker Ballet at the Fischer Theater in Detroit for her and Ashley. Joy had first introduced Sara to the Nutcracker when she was six. It had quickly become a holiday tradition. Last year they had taken Ashley for the first time to a local production. This year was Sara's treat for them. They met her at her apartment, then Sara drove them downtown for lunch and a matinee performance. Sara had been worried about Joy driving all that way and had considered going home for the weekend in order to drive them.

"Don't be silly," Joy had said. "Would all of you stop treating me like I'm an invalid? I'm perfectly capable of driving to Detroit and back."

There had been a scare the day of the Christmas recital. After taking a bow and walking off the stage, Joy had collapsed. When Dale came back stage and saw Joy sitting on a chair drinking water, surrounded by worried dancers, he had thought the worst. His stomach had come up into his throat the same as it had when he had gotten that call back in September. Did she break another bone? Has the cancer spread? Joy waved away the mention of an ambulance. She was fine, she had insisted. It had been a dizzy spell, she insisted – until she threw up in a nearby trash can.

That had turned out to be a simple twenty-four hour bug. Joy's immune system had been compromised by the radiation and chemo she had received in the past. She still wasn't back to full strength. The additional medications were also taking their toll on her immune system. She caught every bug the kids brought home as well as ones from the dance studio. Overdoing it as she prepared for the Christmas recital and Christmas itself had worn her down and made her an easy target for any virus or bug. Joy recuperated on the couch for several days later.

"You have to take better care of yourself," Dale had chided her.

"Yes, doctor," Joy teased.

"You know what I mean. You can't do everything you are used to doing."

"Dale, I am cutting back. If I cut back any more I feel like I would just be existing rather than living." She was happy to let others take care of Christmas for extended family. It was all she could do to take care of her immediate family.

The first drug they had tried didn't seem to be doing what it was supposed to do. The doctor had seemed hopeful that the second one would do the trick. Dale wondered if he would ever stop jumping to conclusions where Joy was concerned. He wondered when he would stop waiting for the next shoe to drop.

Chapter 14

Christmas had been good. Joy had enjoyed seeing the Nutcracker in Detroit with Sara and Ashley. She enjoyed the Christmas Eve service at church and the quiet Christmas morning at home with Dale and the kids before going to her mom's for dinner, but now, she was glad to have it over, glad to focus again on her recovery. She was not happy with her progress. The doctor continued to be hopeful, but she felt something was wrong. She didn't have any energy, was losing weight, didn't have an appetite despite all the tempting foods put before her over the holidays.

"That's to be expected," her doctor informed her. "You're still healing from the hip surgery and you have a cocktail of drugs within you fighting your cancer. You need to rest, to co-operate with the drugs by getting adequate food and rest."

"I am resting," she complained to Dale on the way home. "I'm 'cooperating' with the treatment. If I rest any more, I might as well be dead."

"Joy, don't say that, even in jest," Dale reprimanded her.

"But I don't know what else I can do. I'm doing everything. I'm the ideal patient. I'm just not getting better."

"It takes time. Give it more time," Dale had told her, reassuring himself as much as her. "You are doing everything you are supposed to. We have to continue doing what the doctor says and wait. With time you'll get stronger."

So this is the new normal, she wrote in her blog after getting home. *This is what it is to have a chronic condition, learning to do less, learning how much you can do without over-doing it. I don't like it,* she wrote, ending the post. Sometimes the need to keep blogging felt like just one more drain on her limited energy, one more responsibility. Sometimes she felt it was her saving grace. She knew many people were praying for her, praying for a miracle. She was praying for a miracle too; then she would look at Grace and realize what a miracle that little girl was. She was her miracle baby. Was it too much to ask for another miracle? Perhaps we are only allocated one miracle per lifetime and she already had hers? If so,

she was happy with her miracle. But if God could grant her one more
. . . she wouldn't complain.

She was upset but not surprised when her doctor delivered the
latest update.

"It seems our current course of treatment isn't working any
more. The mets have spread to your lungs and liver." Dale squeezed
Joy's hand. She seemed to be hearing in a vacuum where the
doctor's face zoomed in and out, his voice fading beyond
recognition one minute then screeching in her ear. "Cancer has
spread," it shouted.

"Joy, are you all right?" Dale asked. "Do you understand?"

"What did you say?" Joy asked the doctor to repeat, trying to
hold onto reality, trying to understand what was happening.

"The mets have spread to your lungs and liver," the doctor
repeated.

"And that means?"

"We have to try something new."

"That's not good news," she said quietly.

"No, but there's still hope. It isn't as bad as it sounds."

"It's spread to the lungs and liver."

"Yes."

"Is that why I've been feeling winded lately, and why food
doesn't stay down."

"Not necessarily."

"I thought it was from the drugs."

"It could be. We'll try a new regimen and see what happens."

"Okay." Joy was still in a daze as she drove home in the car
with Dale. The minute she got in the door she went straight to the
play room and picked up Grace, bypassing her mom.

"How did it go?" Mary asked.

"Not good. The mets have spread. The doctor is going to try
some new medications to see if he can halt the spread."

"How is Joy doing?"

"I don't know." They both went into the living room where Joy
was rocking Grace, talking to her and singing.

"Joy, honey, are you okay?" Dale asked.

"No, but I will be."

"Do you want me to stay with you?"

"Do I look like an invalid?" Joy snapped. "Isn't it bad enough that Mom treats me like I'm dying? Not you, too. Go back to work. I'm fine. I've got to get ready for class."

"You know, if you want, you could stay home today," Mary suggested.

"There's no reason for me to stay home, Mom. If I stay home every time I get bad news, I'll never go. I might as well crawl up into a ball and die." Mary was startled by this talk. "I'm no different now than when I left the house this morning, only now I know why I've been so tired." Dale and Mary exchanged glances.

"At least let me drive you," Mary said.

"I can drive myself. Now both of you, get out of here." Joy felt anger rising into her throat. "Go on," she said again, dismissing them. The anger made her feel strangely strong. She refused to acknowledge that anything had changed.

Esther was waiting at the dance studio, anxious to hear what the doctor had said.

"How did it go?" she asked as Joy walked in, Grace and Jacob in tow.

"Not good."

"Not good?" Esther asked.

"I don't want to talk about it." Joy walked down the hall and stopped in front of the painting of her pregnant with Grace, dancing on a high wire. "Get that out of here before I smash it against the wall."

Leticia had joined Esther in the hallway. Both stood in shock at what Joy had said.

"You heard what I said," Joy stated.

"But you love that painting. Sara painted it," Esther started.

"I don't care. I don't want it there leering at me, reminding me of all I once had. Get rid of it or I will."

Esther took the picture off the wall and placed it for safe-keeping in the back seat of her car.

Joy was a whirlwind, teaching her classes, losing herself in her students. Esther called Dale at work. He had been expecting the call.

"What happened?" she asked.

"Joy's cancer has spread to the lungs and liver. How is she?"

"Running around like a banshee. I wondered what had gotten into her. She told me to take Sara's painting down."

"Do you want me to come over?" Dale asked.

"No, not now anyway. I'll let you know if we need you here." Esther hung up and called Kathleen to let her know what had happened.

"I'll be right over," Kathleen said. She didn't know what she could do, but thought she had to at least make an effort.

Joy seemed like her old self, yet with a difference. Where the old Joy always had an under layer of peace and calm even when animated, this one was clearly agitated. Kathleen joined Esther and together they stood outside Joy's room, watching through the glass.

"She told me to take Sara's painting down," Esther said.

"But she loves that painting."

"I know. Said she couldn't bear to look at it."

"That's not like her. What did you do with the picture?"

"In my car. I'll keep it until she comes to her senses." Neither knew what else to say. They both continued in the masquerade of normalcy Joy was perpetuating, waiting for Joy to stop. Joy showed no sign of letting up.

"What do we do?" Kathleen asked.

"I guess we continue as usual until Joy tells us otherwise."

Kathleen stayed as long as she could before leaving for work.

"Are you sure you don't want to go home early?" Esther suggested, hesitantly approaching Joy.

"No, I'm going to live my life as fully as I want for as long as I want, until God tells me otherwise," Joy stated defiantly and went to her next class.

Chapter 15

Their first Christmas as an engaged couple. It had been magical, even with Sara's concerns about Joy. Joy had seemed tired at Christmas dinner, but that was to be expected, Sara had reassured herself.

There was so much to be done for the wedding. They hadn't yet booked a hall or agreed upon a date. Larry wanted to get married in Detroit.

"After all, this is where we live and where we plan to live. Don't you want our married life to begin here?" He had a good point. Sara could hardly argue with that, but every venue they looked at was so expensive. She and Larry didn't have the money. She didn't want to ask her parents to foot the bill, not after all they had already paid for her tuition and other college expenses. Besides, her mom wanted her to hold the wedding in her home town.

"It will be so much easier for me to help if you hold it here. And it would be easier for Joy." That had been a concern for Sara. Then Larry's parents suggested they hold it in his hometown so that put them back in Detroit.

"Why can't we just pick a day and plan from there?" Larry had asked in frustration.

"Because it doesn't work that way," Sara and Anne both assured him. "First you have to pick a venue and see when it is available. The most popular places are booked two years in advance."

"Then I don't want a popular place. I mean, I'm not waiting for two years. I want to get married as soon as possible. I can't wait to start my life with you," he said, giving Sara a kiss.

They were tentatively planning on a fall wedding, right around the time both of their leases expired. That way they could get a place together without breaking a lease. But the venues in Detroit that were available were limited.

"Why not get married here, in your home church?" her dad had suggested over dinner a few weeks ago. "We could rent the hall and have a nice catered meal and it wouldn't cost an arm and a leg."

Sara, her mom and Joy had all given him "that" look and ignored him, going on with their discussion of options.

"I'm just saying, that's what Joy and Dale did and it was a perfectly beautiful wedding." He refused to be shut out of the conversation.

"For us, Dad. That had been right for us. This is Sara's wedding," Joy told her dad.

"What do you think, Larry?" Tom appealed to Larry for support.

"I just want to marry your daughter. I'd be happy to marry her in a barn if that's what she wants," Larry answered.

"That could be arranged," Tom said. "We could put a pole barn up on your property, Dale. What do you think?"

"Sounds like a good idea to me," Dale said, playing along.

"Just ignore them," Joy said with a laugh. "Come on, let's take this conversation elsewhere." They headed for the living room. "I believe it's the men's turn to do the dishes," she added.

"Suit yourself," Dale said, "but just think of the possibility. We could have a hoe down theme, with square dancing and apple bobbing. The bridesmaids' dresses could be those ones you see at square dances, with the big skirts. So could Sara's dress." Dale had been happy to see Joy taking an active part in the discussion about Sara's wedding, smiling as they made plans. It was well worth washing a few dishes to see.

"Now look at where your idea got us, stuck in the kitchen," Tom said.

"Hey, you started it," Dale countered. "Stop complaining."

"I'm not complaining," Tom said as they cleared the table, "But this would have never happened back in my day. The women always knew their place."

"And where was that?" Larry asked.

"Why in the kitchen, of course, baking pie."

"Mmmm, pie ... is there any left?" Larry asked as they finished clearing the table and proceeded to load the dishwasher.

They had finally settled on a venue in Detroit for the third weekend in September, but hadn't signed the contract yet or made a down payment. It overlooked the Detroit River. A former abandoned warehouse that had been rebuilt, it was a little pricey but worth it, they had decided. Besides the owner had given them a break to make it more affordable.

"If we want to be part of the renewal of Detroit, then we need to spend our money in Detroit, supporting local businesses," Larry had convinced her. They were going to finalize the deal that weekend when Sara heard Joy's bad news.

"What does this mean?" she asked her mom.

"We don't know. It's not good, but the doctor has other drugs to try that might work."

"Do you think Joy will be well enough for the wedding?"

"Of course she will be, Sara. Don't let that change your plans."

"But, Mom, if she continues to get worse, she may not be strong enough to come to a September wedding in Detroit, much less help plan it and be in it."

"We'll have no such talk. Of course she will be okay. You can't make your plans on a lot of maybes. Do what's right for you and Larry," Mary had insisted. But how could anything be right for her if Joy couldn't attend. Having Joy at her wedding was more important than any venue, Sara thought.

"Do you think we should move the date up?" she asked Larry.

"This is the earliest opening they have. We were lucky to get this date. The only reason we did was because they had only recently opened up for business. I don't think we can get anything earlier, not that I wouldn't welcome marrying you sooner."

"I just wouldn't want Joy to miss the wedding."

"If I know Joy, she will come even if it means dragging an IV behind her."

"That's not funny," Sara said. Sometimes Larry's sense of humor escaped her. They went ahead with signing the contract and paying the deposit despite Sara's misgivings.

Now with a date in place, the real planning could begin.

Chapter 16

Joy had gotten accustomed to her morning walks with Lucky. As she got stronger she had tried running. The cold air ripped through her lungs. Once she was strong enough to not need help twenty-four/seven she had been reluctant to give up her walk. She had been grateful when her mom offered to watch Grace three mornings a week so she could go for her walk.

Today the cold air felt good as it ripped into her lungs.

"Freeze out that cancer," Joy had thought. There were patches of ice here and there. She skirted them when she saw them, not wanting to stop for anything or anyone, willing herself to keep going. She rounded a curve, hit a patch of ice and fell. Lucky came running over and licked her face.

"Damn," she swore, prepared to lift herself back up, the smell of damp earth filling her nostrils. Instead she started crying, sobbing as warm tears traced her cheeks. Just as before she didn't want to stop running, now that the tears had burst through, she didn't want to stop crying.

"Why me, God? Why me? Why now? Why not later?" she cried.

"God, I know you are there. Answer me." Anger mixed in with the tears, then she said, "God, if you are there, answer me." She sat on the path, not noticing the cold as she sobbed. Then she heard a crackle in the forest, someone, something, was approaching. She stopped crying and listened. Up ahead on the path was a doe. The doe paused and stared into her eyes until two fawns approached. Joy took ahold of Lucky by the collar. Lucky showed no inclination to chase the deer. With one last look, the mother deer picked up her ears as if she heard something, sensed danger, then took off running, her babes close behind.

Joy began to notice the cold of the ground seeping through her clothes. She shivered, got up and proceeded to head back in the direction of her home, this time walking. She wondered about the doe. How had it come so close with a dog present? Was it a sign, she had wondered.

Her anger spent, she went back inside her home to warm up and care for her babies, meeting Jacob as he came off the school bus.

Later that night she related the event to Dale.

"What were you thinking, running in this weather? What if you broke another bone? Who would have heard you in the woods?"

"Mom knew where I was. She would have come looking for me if I were too late getting home. Lucky would have gone for help. Nothing happened. You're missing the point."

"What is the point?"

"The mother deer. I think she was sent to tell me something. I just don't know what."

"Well, there will be no more running in the woods."

"Will it help if I promise you I'll take my cell phone and walk instead of run?"

"No," Dale said then looked at his wife, knowing he would never be able to keep her from doing what she set her mind on. "Okay. No running, just walking, and carry your phone," he agreed. "We'll get through this Joy, just like we got through every problem in the past, together … right? Together?"

Joy agreed as they snuggled under the covers for warmth.

Chapter 17

The wind blew through the city streets. Sara hated driving in Detroit in the winter. There was no money for snow plows so side streets remained snow-covered all winter, creating a slushy, slippery mess.

"Larry, where are you taking me? I thought we had reservations for dinner downtown. We don't want to be late." Reservations on Valentine's Day were hard to come by and not to be taken lightly.

"We won't be," Larry promised. "Isn't this a great neighborhood?"

"You know I love this neighborhood," Sara answered. She had commented to that effect every time they had ridden through or visited friends here. The neighborhood had once been populated by moneyed Detroiters. You turned off a stretch of urban blight with boarded-up businesses, fast cash stores and other small businesses into a whole new world. It was a gem hidden within the wasteland that was Detroit. Row upon row of brownstone houses, all with three stories and carriage houses converted into garages in the back. It had been where the Detroit elite once lived, before fleeing to the suburbs.

It was still a good neighborhood, relatively safe. There were a number of boarded-up houses for sale as owners defaulted on loans, but overall the area was booming in comparison to other parts of Detroit.

Larry pulled up to one such house. "What do you think?"

"What do I think?" Sara looked at the outside of a brown stone with boarded-up windows. It looked like it had potential, appeared to be solidly built.

"Come in. Look it over," Larry said, opening her side of the car, stepping in piles of sludge.

"I can't."

"Sure you can." Larry took hold of her arm and escorted her to the house.

A Realtor opened the side door for them. The house was chilled and empty of furniture. Wallpaper hung loose from the wall in places.

"We are just keeping enough heat in here to keep the pipes from bursting," the Realtor said, "Sorry." She knew it was not the ideal situation for selling a home.

"That's okay," Larry assured her. "It's in foreclosure," he told Sara as he gave her the tour. "Do you mind if we look by ourselves?"

"There's nothing worth stealing in this house. I guess it won't hurt."

There was a nice sized kitchen, though outdated and in need of work, a large pantry, living room, dining room, sun room and half a bath on the first floor. There were three large bedrooms, two bathrooms and a spacious stairway, landing and halls on the second floor.

Larry took her hand and led her up the flight of stairs to the third floor.

"This is the best part of all," he said. "Close your eyes."

He took her up the final steps. "Open your eyes," he told her. The third floor was one large room, with windows on all four sides and a sloping roof on two sides.

"I thought this would make an awesome art studio for you."

Sara walked about the room, gazed out the windows on the snow-covered streets below. A soft light was filtering through one set of windows from the street lights below and the moon above.

"It's nice," she said, "but, really, how much work does the house need? Can we afford it?"

"It needs a lot of work, but that's why we can afford it. Dale could help with the plumbing. The wiring needs to be checked, but my uncle is an electrician. He'll do it for us for a reasonable price. We'll need insulation but I believe the furnace is still functional. The house is structurally sound. I mean, all the other repairs are superficial: paint, wall paper, maybe some dry wall patching. What do you think?" Larry paused in his ramblings.

"It's very big."

"Lots of room for kids and guests," he began again. "There's even an apartment above the carriage house. We could rent it to help with the bills. Maybe Anne would want to live there. The house is big enough she could even stay in one of our spare bedrooms."

"It will take so much furniture to fill the place."

"Your mom and my mom both love garage sales. They'll have this place full of furniture in no time, and have a ball doing it. We can take care of the wallpaper and painting ourselves."

"It will be so much work to keep clean."

"But we're young. We can do it. And it's a good neighborhood. You said so yourself. Other couples from work live here. There's a neighborhood association, a number of young families are moving in. Won't it be a great place to raise children?" Larry paused to give Sara time to take it all in.

"And besides, just think of this studio. Wouldn't that be great?" he added.

Sara was thinking about the studio. She could see herself up there, painting, sketching. With windows on all sides she would get the morning light and evening light. It was almost ideal.

"Are you sure we can afford it?"

"We've got two incomes."

"I know, and two sets of student loans," Sara interrupted.

Larry continued, ignoring what Sara had said, "Besides, it's a bargain. There are lots of bargains in Detroit just waiting to be scooped up, but not as many in this neighborhood. I mean we can be part of the revitalizing of Detroit." Sara was trying to resist Larry's enthusiasm and remain practical, but it was a losing battle.

"I know," she finally said, "but I want my dad and Dale to look at it first before we sign anything. And my mom and Joy, and your mom." Sara looked around the room with a smile as she imagined bringing Joy here. "Joy is going to love this," she said.

"And my uncle."

"And your dad."

"So, it's a done deal?" Larry asked.

"A maybe." That was enough for Larry. He picked her up and swung her around. "Happy Valentine's Day," he said. Together they ran down the open staircase to where the Realtor waited below.

"We'll be in touch," Larry assured her before leaving. They proceeded to their dinner, but both of their minds were back in the house.

Chapter 18

"Hey, baby brother," Josh said, putting a headlock on Scott and rubbing the top of his head before sitting down next to him. "What's for lunch?" He reached over and grabbed one of Scott's potato chips. Scott hated it when Josh referred to him as "baby".

"Same as what you have." Scott and Josh had been packing their own lunches since they were old enough to express their preferences, and complaints, to their grandmother.

"You can pack your own lunch if you don't like what I fix," Esther had told them. She made sure there were plenty of portable options available for them to choose from, lunch meat, cheese, peanut butter for sandwiches, fruits and cut up vegetables, snack size bags of chips, cookies and Twinkies. She had long stopped supervising their lunch-making efforts. The arrival of their mom hadn't changed this. At one point that first year after Katherine had come home, she had gotten up and gotten in their way while they fixed their lunches, offering to help.

"We've got this, Mom. Just sit down and drink your coffee," Josh had told her. Kathleen had been happy to get out of their way.

"What are you doing here? This isn't your lunch hour? Don't you have class?" Scott asked.

"Just wanted to let you know I'm going to be staying late after practice. Coach wants us to go over some more videos. Tell mom and grandma for me." Josh didn't wait for a response. He looked over at Steven and Ralph.

"Ralph, Steven, right?" he said, reaching over and shaking their hands. "I'm Josh." He introduced himself. "I'm glad to see you're keeping my kid brother out of trouble," he said as he stood up. He barely acknowledged Stephanie as he prepared to leave. "Gotta go. Can't be late for physics," he said as he grabbed a carrot stick from Scott. "See ya."

"So that's your brother?" Stephanie commented. "The great basketball player."

"Yeah, well . . ." Scott started.

"Full of himself, isn't he?"

"Nah, he's okay," Scott said then dropped the subject. He didn't want Stephanie to fall under Josh's spell like his other female friends. Josh didn't try to do this. It just happened.

Stephanie and Scott had become friends after bonding over the incident in the cafeteria. The fact that their parents had forbidden it made it all the sweeter—forbidden fruit. They had passed notes to each other back and forth, during detention, and shared homework. They also made a point of befriending Ralph and Steven, sitting with them during lunch hours in order to keep away Warren and his friends.

"So, it's pretty cool, what you're doing," Josh told Scott when he got home from practice that night. Scott was sitting at the kitchen table doing homework. Josh pulled out leftovers from the refrigerator and put them in the microwave.

"What are you talking about?"

"I saw how you were eating with Ralph and Steven today."

"It's no big deal. They're my friends."

"Call it what you want. I think it's great."

"Okay, thanks," Scott said to get Josh to forget about it and not say anything else. He didn't want attention for what he was doing. He wasn't doing it for attention. He didn't want it made into a big deal at Ralph and Steven's expense. He was doing it because it was the right thing and because Stephanie was doing it. No reason for acclamation.

"You know, if anybody gives you a hard time, let me know. I'll take care of them."

"Yeah, sure." That was something he didn't want, Josh fighting his battles. It was hard enough living in his shadow without adding insult.

"So who was the girl you were with?"

"Nobody," Scott said.

"What girl?" Erick asked as he came into the kitchen for a snack.

"No one," Scott continued. He was glad his mom wasn't there to quiz him. There were definitely advantages to her working evenings.

"Just asking. She was cute," Josh teased.

"Doesn't anybody care that I've got homework to do," Josh said as he picked up his books. "I'm going to my room."

"But you can't hide. Remember, we share the same room."

"Like I could ever forget," Scott grunted as he headed up the stairs.

It was bad enough that he had to share a room with his brother. Must he also share his friends? He wasn't about to tell Josh about Stephanie.

Stephanie, for her part, feigned disinterest where Josh was concerned. She had seen him coming out of his math class as she was going in to hers. He was in college prep courses, like her, just two years ahead. She couldn't miss him in his team shirt on game days. She wasn't a great fan of basketball but if anyone could make her a fan, it was him, she thought.

Chapter 19

Joy loved the house as much as Sara had imagined, though she wasn't able to make it up all of the stairs into the third floor.

"I'd love your suggestions as far as paint, wallpaper and curtains," Sara said.

"That you will get. It's a beautiful building," Joy was enjoying her day out in the big city. Esther and Kathleen were watching the kids to give them this day off. Dale was checking out the plumbing throughout the house, flushing each toilet, running water in every sink and tub, checking for leaks, seeing which pipes needed to be replaced.

"Seems to be pretty sound," Dale said.

Larry's parents and his uncle met them at the house as well.

"I'm afraid you are looking at a major rewiring," Larry's uncle said. "Looks like the wiring hasn't been updated for decades. Best to just redo all of it. Otherwise there's the risk of fire. I'll figure out what I need and let you know." He made notations on a clipboard. "The labor will be my wedding gift to you," he told them.

This was their first chance to get Larry's and Sara's parents together. After touring the house they went to the wedding venue and ended up at a Greek restaurant for an early dinner.

Larry and Sara had already made an offer on the house. Now it was just a matter of seeing whether the bank would accept their offer and whether their credit came through for a home loan. Both sets of parents were helping with the down payment. As long as there were no major snags along the way it looked like Larry and Sara would be homeowners by spring and able to start on the necessary repairs.

Towards the end of the meal, Joy began to feel queasy. "Are you okay?" Dale whispered.

"A little weak."

"Do you want to leave?"

"I think so." Dale knew that if Joy admitted she needed to leave that meant she was feeling worse than she would admit. Ordinarily Joy would insist she was okay no matter how tired she was.

"I'm so sorry, but we won't be able to stay for dessert," Dale said, standing up. Mary and Tom had been enjoying their conversation with Larry's parents and hadn't noticed how pale Joy looked. One look told them all they needed to know. They quickly prepared to leave. Tom asked for the bill but Larry's dad intervened.

"My treat," he said with a smile. "It's been a pleasure meeting you. You get that young lady home. It's been a long day."

"Yes, it has. Long but a good one," Mary said as all stood up and exchanged pleasantries before leaving.

Sara watched with fear as Dale helped Joy out of the restaurant.

"I don't want dessert," she said as others ordered. "But you go ahead," she told them. Larry and his parents and uncle ordered desserts.

"I'm sorry we didn't have more time with your family, Sara," Larry's mom said. "They are lovely people. Larry told us about Joy's cancer. Said it had spread. So sad. Such a nice young woman."

"Yeah, right," Sara agreed, finding it hard to focus on the conversation. It was a relief to finally be home back at her apartment after saying goodbye to Larry's family.

"Just think, soon we'll own our first house," Larry said with excitement. When Sara didn't respond he asked, "What's wrong?"

"I'm worried about Joy. Did you see how tired she looked?"

"It was a long day for everyone, Sara. I'm sure it's nothing more than that," Larry tried to reassure her.

Once Larry left, Sara called and talked to Dale.

"How is Joy?"

"She's in bed. It was a big day for her."

"Is she really okay?"

"As okay as she can be given the circumstances. I wish I could tell you more."

"You will tell me, won't you? If anything happens. If she gets worse. Promise."

"Promise," Dale said. Don't make promises you can't keep. He remembered his mom telling him that when he was a kid, maybe Ashley's age or a little older. Back then promises had come easy. He promised all kinds of things, never counting the cost, not knowing the cost.

"Pinky swear," he would promise his friends.

Was this a promise he couldn't keep? What if this promise conflicted with another promise, a prior promise to Joy? What to do then?

He had made a promise to Joy when they had married. How little had they both known where that promise would take them, what was in store for them. But a promise was a promise. He would love her till death do them part and beyond that. This he knew.

He had also promised her to be true to her, be honest even when it hurt, even when it was hard. That was one promise he couldn't keep. Sometimes a lie was better than the truth.

Joy woke up when he slid into bed. "Sorry, I didn't mean to wake you."

"It doesn't take much some days."

"Sara called. She's worried about you."

"I know. I could tell. You didn't tell her anything?"

"No, but it's hard to keep up this pretense. We have to tell her. We can't keep lying."

"If she knew, she would cancel all of her wedding plans just so I could attend. I want her to have the wedding of her dreams."

"Even if that doesn't include you?"

"It may still include me. We don't know anything for sure. You aren't getting rid of me that easy."

"You have to tell her. It should be her decision," Dale wasn't being put off. "It's her right to change her plans. Besides, she's going to find out. How much longer can you keep on as if nothing were happening?"

"I'll keep on as long as I can."

The news at Joy's latest doctor appointment continued to be less than positive. The mets were still spreading, just not as fast as they had been. The drugs hadn't stopped all of the growth.

"We still have options," the doctor said.

"And when we run out of options?" she had asked.

"We'll deal with that when it happens, though you might want to think about what kind of care you want if the cancer continues to spread. Do you want information on Hospice?"

Dale waited for Joy to answer. It was her call.

Finally Joy said, "Yes, I would." The doctor gave them some information and phone numbers to call for more information.

Dale hid the papers in his briefcase where they remained his and Joy's secret. Just between the two of them.

Chapter 20

Joy shuffled through the mail, stopping at a stray bill from a medical company, Pathology Associates. She opened the bill and saw it was from the pathologist who had read her most recent biopsy. She wasn't surprised at the bill. What surprised her was that this was the first one she had seen. When she had asked Dale before about medical bills, he had assured her that they were taken care of. She hadn't pursued it any further since she had been so busy with rehab, trying to regain strength, the dance studio, Christmas and the kids. It had struck her as funny that she hadn't received any bills or statements from the insurance company but had believed Dale when he said they were taken care of. Now she began to wonder. How were they being taken care of?

She waited till the kids were in bed before confronting Dale with the bill.

"Dale," she asked as she handed him the bill, "Where are the other medical bills?"

"They're being taken care of."

"That's not what I asked. Where are they? I want to see them."

"They aren't here, if that's what you mean."

"Then where are they?"

Dale fidgeted in his chair, unable to meet her penetrating gaze.

"Kathleen has them," he finally said, "at least the ones that are still due. The others are at my office. I don't want you to worry about them."

"Why does Kathleen have them? She doesn't need to know our business."

"She offered to help. I was taking care of them myself but it got to be so complicated."

"But . . ." Joy tried to interrupt Dale.

"There were multiple bills for the same procedure. Bills from the doctor, the pathologist, charges for the facility, the drugs." Joy kept trying to interrupt Dale's monologue with no success. "I decided to take Kathleen up on her offer. She's good at multi-tasking, handling all of the loose ends. She doesn't get as frustrated as I was getting," he finally stopped.

"But why didn't you give them to me to take care of like I always have?"

"I wanted to give you a break."

"I'm so tired of people treating me like I'm a porcelain doll about to break. I'm not fragile, Dale. I haven't got my foot in the grave, not yet anyway. Stop treating me like I am. Let me keep doing what I can for as long as I can." Joy's voice rose with her irritation.

"But remember how frustrated you got with the bills the last time."

"I did fine."

"It's practically a full time job," Dale ignored her. "Keeping the bills straight, checking charges, dealing with the insurance and right billing codes. Kathleen's doing a great job."

"And I didn't?"

"No, that's not what I meant."

"It wasn't for you to decide."

"And what about you not letting Sara know about your condition? You are deciding for her." Dale tried to divert the argument away from him, going on the offensive.

"That's not the same, and you know it."

"Do I? How is it different?"

"It just is," Joy realized she was on shaky ground but refused to budge. "So how much have we paid and how much do we owe?"

"Several thousand," Dale said.

"Is that how much we have spent or how much we owe?"

"Both. I don't have the exact figures with me, but you can see the check book for the ones I already paid." Dale brought out his checkbook.

"When did you open a separate checking account?"

"When you were first diagnosed with breast cancer and I didn't want you to worry about money."

"But, this doesn't make sense. I took care of all of the bills back then."

"Not all of them," Dale said. "There were some I intercepted and paid."

"And when were you going to tell me about this?"

"Never," he said, "or at least not until they were all paid and you were cancer-free. I set up a payment schedule with the hospital for the bills from your surgery. I told them to send the bills to my office. I don't know how this one slipped through."

"It's a good thing it did." Joy sat down with her head in her hand as she tried to take this in.

"I know how you worry about money. I don't want you worrying about the cost of your treatment. I just want you to get better." Dale reached for her hands and tried to make eye contact.

Joy wasn't sure what to think. Her mind was cloudy from the drugs, making it hard to think clearly. Finally she said, "I want to see all of the bills," stated through clenched teeth.

"Kathleen has them."

"Have her bring them over here tomorrow morning. I want to know exactly just how much all of this treatment is costing. Maybe there are things I can do without."

"That's precisely what I was afraid you would say." His voice began to rise.

"I won't have my illness bankrupting my family, putting my children's future in jeopardy." Joy's voice rose to meet Dale's.

"It's not. That's what we have insurance for. And I won't have you skimping on medical care you need to save a penny," Dale shouted.

Just then Ashley came down stairs, followed by Lucky.

"Mommy, Daddy, I heard yelling. Is everything all right?"

"Sure it is honey, Mommy and Daddy are just having a discussion," Joy said.

"I don't like your discussion," Ashley said.

"Everything's all right," Dale said. "Go back to bed. Mommy and I were just getting ready to go to bed ourselves. Weren't we?" Dale got a glass of water for Ashley and took her back upstairs.

"This isn't finished," Joy said as they went to bed.

"I know," Dale said. It was the first time they hadn't been able to work out a problem before they want to sleep. The first time they went to bed angry. They had had plenty of disagreements in the past but somehow managed to put them behind them before they went to bed even if it meant long hours and little to no sleep. Dale didn't like this, but he didn't know what he could do.

Chapter 21

Kathleen brought over all the medical bills and records as ordered by Joy.

Joy was surprised at how many expenses remained after insurance. Everything was organized. Kathleen had done a good job staying on top of everything. Joy appreciated that. She also begrudgingly admitted that she would have had a hard time doing all that Kathleen had done.

"Thank you," Joy said. "I appreciate your help with this, but now it's time for me to take this over." Even as she said this, she knew it was a mistake. She didn't have the energy to deal with it, but she didn't want to burden Kathleen or Dale with it either.

"Let me do it, Joy. It's such a small thing. There is so little that I can do to help. Let me do this. I'm happy to do it. I even seem to be good at it. It's like a numbers game, playing the numbers to get the best deal, to make sure you are getting everything you are entitled to. They don't go out of their way to help people with this, the insurance company and hospitals." Joy considered her offer.

"Tell me, Kathleen - how has Dale been managing all these bills? He never once told me we needed to cut back on expenses or even to be careful with money, even at Christmas time."

"He doesn't want you to know," Kathleen looked at Joy then figured she had a right to know. "He took out a loan on his business to cover the expenses. He didn't want you to know because you would have said no, but it's not that much. His business can handle it. You'll be okay financially." Joy sat and took all of this in. She didn't know what to say.

"Kathleen, I don't know what to do. I've always pulled my own weight. Sure, I don't make as much money as Dale but I contributed to the household. Now I feel like a burden. And it may get worse. I don't want to put Dale or the kids through this."

"What are you talking about?" Kathleen asked.

"All this … haven't they suffered enough? It was different when I had some hope of recovery, regaining my full strength. Now it seems all I have to look forward to is getting weaker, being a burden to my family and piling up bills. That's not a life. That's not the legacy I want to leave my family," Joy's voice broke as tears surfaced.

"Joy, how can you say that? You aren't a burden."

"Maybe not so much now, but I will be."

"Is there something you and Dale haven't told me?"

Joy pushed the papers asides, handing them to Kathleen.

"I'm dying, Kathleen. Maybe not today, maybe not tomorrow, maybe not this year, but I am. Dale doesn't want to admit it. The doctor still holds out hope. I want to hold onto that hope too. But sometimes, I just have to face the truth. I don't have the ten years or more that I had hoped for. I don't want to bankrupt my family. I don't want to steal from my children's future."

Kathleen sat in silence, unwilling to accept what she already knew in her heart.

"Are you all right?" Joy asked when Kathleen continued in silence.

"I'm okay, I guess," Kathleen finally responded, struggling to hold back tears. "I'm sorry, I'm just not ready to accept this, but this isn't about me. It's about you."

"That's just the problem. Everything is about me, doing everything possible to help me without a thought about how much it costs. What if the price is too high?"

"It's not," Kathleen assured her. "I've seen Dale's financials. Your family will be okay."

"It's not just about money," Joy stared out past Kathleen to the window beyond her. "I understand why some people want to take this into their own hands."

"Joy, you're not thinking about assisted suicide?"

"No, of course not," Joy paused, lowered her head, then pretended to be reading through the papers again, "but if I were," she looked up, directly into Kathleen's eyes, "would you be willing to help?"

"Joy, don't talk like that. You still have time ahead for you, good days, good months. I won't listen anymore, can't listen anymore."

"But when and if the time comes, could I talk to you then?" Joy didn't know who else she could talk to about this. Certainly not Dale, or Sara, or her mom. Kathleen was the only one she could talk to rationally about this. Even Kathleen found the conversation difficult.

"If the time comes, we can talk," Kathleen finally said.

"That's all I ask. I just want to know I have someone I can talk to." Kathleen didn't know why Joy trusted her with this knowledge. She felt both honored that she would share this with her, and terrified at the possibility. Why did she have to be the one to carry this additional burden?

As if knowing what Kathleen was thinking, Joy said, "You are strong, Kathleen. Stronger than you realize." Joy pulled out the information the doctor had given her on Hospice.

"I'm thinking about contacting Hospice. The doctor gave us this information and phone numbers. I just don't know. I don't want to do this too soon. I have to have a terminal diagnosis to enter Hospice. I also want to know how much it will cost."

"Do you want me to check it out for you?"

"If you would, that would be great. I don't know that I can handle it just yet. You'll tell me everything you find out, won't you?" she asked, handing Kathleen the brochure.

"Of course," Kathleen agreed as she accepted the information. "And would you let me continue to take care of the medical bills?"

"Yes." That was a relief to Joy. She knew she couldn't do it, just found it hard to admit. "But I want to see everything."

"That you will. I'll give you a regular report, weekly if you want. You'll be able to see everything." Kathleen assured her.

"I was so mean to Dale last night. I was so angry at him. I don't know why. I just don't want to be treated like a helpless child," Joy changed the subject, again looking out the window.

"I'm sure he meant well." Kathleen reached for Joy's hand.

"I know. He always means well, but he was wrong."

"I think he realizes that."

"I don't want him or anyone to count me out until I can no longer do what I do. Does that make sense? I don't want to die while I'm still alive."

"Makes all the sense in the world," Kathleen said, continuing to hold Joy's hand. "What about telling Esther about Hospice? And others?"

"Not yet. Not yet. I'll know when it's time. There will be time enough in the future, what future I have left."

Chapter 22

Sara had her dress picked out and ordered. A beautiful, ivory white, sleeveless dress. The seamstress assured her that the bodice would hold her breasts, avoiding a wardrobe malfunction.

"We can't have the girls escaping," the seamstress stated as Sara shook her shoulders, testing that promise.

Sara had decided on simple grey cocktail dresses for her bridesmaids, with several options to choose from. That way they weren't forced into a one-style-fits-all but could pick the style that looked best on them. They also wouldn't be stuck with a formal dress they would never wear again.

She had already ordered her Save-the-Date cards and was preparing to send them out the first of April. They hadn't decided yet on the invitation but figured they still had plenty of time to get them printed and ready for mailing in July. Everything was falling into place. They had closed on the house and were in the process of picking paint and wallpaper. Sara was busy and happy.

Her mom was coming to Detroit for her dress fitting. Afterwards they were going to lunch. She had been disappointed that Joy couldn't join her and the other bridesmaids but understood. When Sara asked her mom how Joy was doing, her face darkened and she turned aside.

"What's wrong, Mom?"

Her mom smiled, "Nothing, honey, this is your day. Let's not spoil it."

"Spoil it? How will talking about Joy spoil it?"

"They are talking about bringing in Hospice."

"Hospice? I mean, really…?"

"They are just talking. Joy is still going to the dance studio every day, working on the recital."

"Then it can't be so bad." Sara tried to reassure herself.

"Yes, dear. Let's talk about happier things."

When Sara related the conversation to Larry that night he suggested it was time for her to go home and see for herself. They made plans to go that Saturday.

Sara was surprised at how skinny Joy was. Joy had always been skinny. She couldn't afford to lose any weight.

"It seems no matter how much I eat, I can't gain any weight."

"That's a good problem to have, I guess," Sara said. At another time she would have commented on how jealous she was, how she just looked at desserts and gained weight. Didn't seem funny today.

"Joy, why didn't you tell me?" she finally asked.

"Tell you what?"

"Tell me you were considering Hospice."

"Who told you?" Joy avoided Sara's gaze, turning aside as if by doing so she could avoid the question.

"Mom, of course."

"I told her not to say anything."

"Really, how long were you going to keep this from me?" Sara took Joy's hands, trying to get her to look at her.

"I didn't want to spoil your wedding. This is your big day. I don't want anything to interfere with that." Joy continued to look away.

"And you didn't think the possibility that you would not be able to attend wouldn't spoil the day?" Sara said.

"That had been pointed out to me." She looked over at Dale.

"And you, you promised you would tell me," Sara gave Dale an accusatory look.

"Blame me, not Dale. It was all my idea," Joy said.

"Do you have an estimate of how much time you have left?" Sara asked softly, afraid to say the words out loud.

"Oh, Sara, don't be so dramatic. I'm not dead yet. I still might have years," Joy stated, finally looking at her sister.

"The doctor says her mets don't seem to be responding to any of the drugs they have tried so far. We seem to be running out of options," Dale informed her.

"But that's for another day. For today we have happier things to occupy our time. How are the wedding plans coming?" Joy asked changing the subject.

Sara told her about the plans, but with little enthusiasm. Larry and she stayed overnight with her parents and went to their church with them. Larry liked the church, though it was larger than he was used to.

Sara took Larry aside afterwards. "What about moving the wedding up to June and having it here?" she asked him.

"But we will lose our down payment."

"I know, but I don't think we can wait." They approached the minister but unfortunately there were no open dates for weddings in June.

"Maybe you could have the wedding at Dale and Joy's church?" her mother suggested when they told her parents about what had happened.

They called the church and were able to meet the pastor that afternoon. Larry liked the church immediately. It was closer to what he was used to.

"I mean, our wedding party would have been lost in that huge church," he said. They were expecting around two hundred.

They checked the church calendar and were able to schedule the wedding for Father's Day weekend.

When asked about officiating at the wedding, Pastor Joe paused. He usually required six month's advance notice before a wedding for pre-marriage preparation. He wasn't sure how they would be able to fit it in given such a short amount of time, but when he looked at Sara, he couldn't say no. The family resemblance was evident. He was well aware of Joy's situation.

Sara and Larry contacted his parents and the rest of the bridal party about the date and place change, but they didn't tell Joy and Dale. They cancelled their Detroit site and caterer, losing their deposit, revised their Save-the-Dates, and sent them out as soon as they got them back. That was how Joy and Dale found out about the change.

Joy looked at the card in surprise. She called Dale at work.

"Dale, did you know anything about this?" she asked.

"About what?"

"Sara's wedding. The date's been changed to June and it is being held at our church."

"This is the first I've heard it," he said.

When Joy asked her mom, her mom just said, "She told me not to say anything."

"I guess Sara will do what she wants to do," Dale said when he got home. Joy just shook her head.

"I hope she didn't do this because of me."

"And if she did," Dale said, "it was her decision to make."

Chapter 23

"Why isn't this covered? But they've met the deductible already . . .
I thought it was supposed to pay at eighty percent, not fifty percent .
. . So I have to call the doctor's office about the code?"

"You're telling me you have nothing to do with billing, but
billing is telling me to contact you."

"I feel like I'm being given the run-around . . . Who am I
talking to . . . Look, Joyce, let me talk to your supervisor . . ."

"What are you doing?" Esther asked. Kathleen had been on the
phone for the past hour. Esther caught bits and pieces of the
conversation as she came in and out of the kitchen.

"I'm trying to find out why the insurance didn't pay more of
Joy's latest bill." Kathleen had a notebook in front of her where she
noted each phone call, who she spoke with and what transpired.

Esther glanced at the notations. "Pretty impressive," she
commented as she went through the notebook. There were pages of
records.

"You have to keep on top of this stuff," Kathleen said. "The
insurance companies aren't out to make it easy. I write down every
contact so I have a record and the name of who said what. You'd be
surprised at the conflicting information I get at times. No one seems
to know what the other one is doing. They pass the buck from one
place to another. I shuffle back between insurance, the doctor's
office, billing. No wonder most people just give up and pay these
bills without question. It's practically a full-time job. Dale doesn't
have time to deal with this. The phone calls need to be made during
the day. Sometimes you can be on hold for twenty minutes or more."

Esther was impressed. Not only was Kathleen working the
system, she wasn't getting upset through the process. Esther would
have been angry and frustrated long before this.

"You know, there probably is a market for this."

"For what?"

"For what you are doing. People would be happy to pay you to
straighten out all their medical bills."

"But wouldn't that be taking advantage of someone's
misfortune? I couldn't do that. I know I haven't lived the best life,

but even I have some standards. I wouldn't take advantage of someone struggling with medical bills."

"Well, there's a need. Whenever there's a need there's someone ready to exploit that need."

"Not me," Kathleen stated, but the seed had been planted.

That Sunday, over dinner, Esther filled in Peter about what Kathleen was doing.

"There are plenty of people dealing with multiple medical bills that get frustrated and quit. Especially senior citizens. They could use an advocate," Peter said. "My mom for one. What would you charge?"

"I can't charge someone for doing what I'm doing for Joy and Dale," Kathleen countered. She wasn't sure about having Peter, her former probation officer, knowing so much about her life. She had received a new probation officer when her mom had started dating him, but he was still a probation officer and knew her new one.

"If you want to learn about medical billing, there are courses at the community college," Esther suggested.

"I don't want to be a medical transcriptionist, dealing with billing all day long, punching numbers."

"You could use the information to help you help others," Esther continued.

"You know, you don't have to charge for it," Peter suggested. "You could start a non-profit to provide this service to seniors and others with health issues. The non-profit would pay your salary. You won't make a lot of money, especially at first, but you could make a decent living and help others in the process."

"But how would I start?" Kathleen asked.

"Mom, you could do crowd-funding for it," Josh chimed in.

"What's crowd funding?" Erick asked, joining the conversation.

"It's a new thing on the internet, Grandpa," Josh answered. "It's a way to raise money for a new venture. You put your proposal on the internet and people contribute to it. It would be a good way to see if there is any interest."

"Kind of like putting it up the flagpole and seeing if anyone salutes," Erick said.

"Precisely," Peter laughed at the saying.

"I'm in," Erick said. "I'd support an idea like that. Where do I sign up?"

"My mom could be your first client," Peter said.

"You could use the office at Joy's that had been set aside for Sara. No one is using it," Esther added.

"It sounds like it's already settled," Peter said.

"We'll see," Kathleen said, pausing to finish the last bite of her dinner, "It will take a lot of time and energy."

"Something you have in abundance," Esther said.

"Okay, I'll think about it," Kathleen said, ending the discussion. She continued to think about the idea that night. Maybe it could work. She needed a cause, Joy had said, maybe this was it. She would have to learn about setting up a non-profit, would need to file for a 501c3. Challenging, but she liked a challenge. Besides, as an ex-felon, this was her best chance for getting a decent job outside of the fast food industry. Even with a degree, employers were hesitant to hire anyone with a record. Being an entrepreneur might be the best way to go.

"Sounds like a good idea to me. How are you going to fund this?" her probation officer told her when she told him about the idea.

"Donations. I've already got a commitment for $5,000 through crowd funding."

Chapter 24

Kathleen arranged for Dale and Joy to meet with the social worker and a nurse from Hospice to discuss options.

"To receive Hospice benefits you have to have a six-month life expectancy, but that doesn't mean you are required to die on schedule in six months. Often people receive such good care with Hospice that they live longer than expected." Kathleen explained.

"Yes, sometimes they have to go off Hospice for a while but can always be added back on. They call it 'failure to die,' " the nurse added.

"Yes, well my friend Charlene's husband went with Hospice and died the next day." It was Mary's morning to watch Grace. Kathleen had hoped she would stay out of this, but apparently not. Mary brought Grace into the living room and was watching her while listening in.

"That's probably because they waited too long," the nurse stated. "Unfortunately, many people wait until the last minute to bring in Hospice, which means they don't get the full benefit of what Hospice can provide." Kathleen had already told this to Joy and Dale but thought it was good for them to hear it again from someone associated with Hospice. Kathleen had done her homework, checking out the different Hospice options that had sprung up in their town over the last few years. Kathleen found her efforts to help Dale and Joy dovetailed nicely with her new business. She was able to use what she had learned helping Joy for her business and was able to use what she was researching for her business to help Joy and Dale. She was still developing the business in her mind, but had already taken on her first client, Peter's mom, on a trial basis.

"The other requirement is that you not be seeking a cure, only comfort care. Your doctor is already treating this as a chronic condition, not curable, so you meet that criteria," Kathleen added. She had already told them this, trying to convince both about the benefit of Hospice. Joy was already on board with this. Dale was hesitant but he had agreed to this meeting and arranged for the time off from work.

"Yes, Hospice only provides palliative care - that is comfort care. You can't be actively seeking a cure under Hospice," the nurse confirmed this, "but what you will receive is the best possible care for pain and discomfort to increase the quality of life."

"We focus more on quality of life rather than quantity," the social worker jumped in. "Besides medical care, we help with other aspects of the dying process." Dale and Mary both started at the sound of the last words. "We provide social, emotional, spiritual, legal help. We are here to help you with every aspect of dying." She said it again, Dale thought. He didn't want to hear any more. Joy listened attentively, asking questions and trying to take it all in.

"So, you help maneuver through the medical system, helping with services and insurance. How is that different from what Kathleen is already doing for me?" Joy asked.

"They won't be taking over what I'm doing, but will help me navigate the system," Kathleen explained.

"We also monitor your prescription and pain meds to make sure you are getting the full benefit from them," the nurse said.

"We can help you navigate social services and help with legal questions, funeral arrangements," the social worker stated. "And we have a chaplain available as well."

"We have our own minister," Joy said.

"The chaplain isn't there to replace your minister. He has special expertise and experience with death and dying and can help with spiritual issues, but only if you want him to. Just because a service is available to you through Hospice, doesn't mean you have to use it. We have a whole range of options," the social worker continued.

"We can provide respite care to give your caregivers a break," the nurse added.

"That won't be necessary. I can take care of my daughter. We have plenty of help. We don't need any strangers in our home," Mary said abruptly, no longer able to hold her tongue. "I'm sure you people do a lot of good for those who need you, but as you can see, my daughter isn't dying and when and if she is, we can take care of her." Mary began to dismiss the women.

"Mary, this isn't your decision to make but Joy and Dale's," Kathleen said. Kathleen looked to Dale for support but Dale refused to say anything.

Finally Joy said, "Thank you for your time. We have your number. We'll call you if we need any more information."

Kathleen walked the women to the door. "I'm sorry. I think they just need more time," she said.

"Don't worry about it," the social worker said. "We're used to such reactions. Feel free to call us if you need any more information or if you need our services."

Back in the living room, Mary was spouting off. "The idea. Whose idea was it to bring in an outside organization? We can take care of our own. We don't need any outsiders interfering with our business. Besides, you aren't dying, Joy. If you need someone to talk to, I can contact our pastor."

"We have our own pastor, Mom," Joy said, looking at Dale. He remained silent. "Dale, what do you think?" Dale refused to meet her eyes.

"I need to get back to work," he said.

"Okay," Joy said. "We can talk about this later," she said.

"Yeah, sure," he said as he gave her a kiss.

Kathleen stopped Dale on his way out. "Dale, what's up?"

"I can't believe you brought those people into our home."

"It wasn't my idea. It was Joy's idea. I thought you two had talked about this."

"We have, we did. I just didn't think it would be like this."

"Like what?" Dale tried to get past her and out the door, but Kathleen wouldn't let him, standing in his way.

"Like what?" she repeated.

"She's not dying," Dale shouted between his teeth, not wanting Joy to hear him. He stepped outside with Kathleen following.

"Yes, she is," Kathleen said quietly, touching his arm. "You know that, don't you?"

"No, I don't and neither do you, or Joy or those women. They don't know. No one knows the day or hour, only God knows. I won't listen anymore."

"But Dale, she is. You don't want her dying alone."

"She won't die alone. She's not dying."

"She will die alone if you refuse to admit it and talk to her about it." Kathleen and Joy had had many opportunities to talk about dying during her weekly visits. Even though Dale had agreed to consider Hospice, she knew he had yet to accept the possibility of her dying.

"I have to get to work," Dale insisted, pulling away from her hand and getting into his car.

Inside the house, Mary was still going on about the women from Hospice.

"I can't believe you invited those women into your home."

"I did, Mom, and they will be back. You don't have any say in the matter," Joy told her.

"I don't have any say in the matter? So I'm supposed to just show up, take care of my grandbabies and shut up?"

"That would be good, Mom. Now, if you don't mind, I need a nap before going to the studio." Joy dismissed her mom.

"Thank you," she said to Kathleen as she went upstairs. "See you tomorrow?" she asked.

"Yes, call me if you need me."

Kathleen hadn't been surprised at Mary's reaction, but she was surprised at Dale's. He, more than anyone, should be aware of what was happening to his wife. He and Joy had always seemed joined at the hip. If they ever had a disagreement, it had not been evident to her. But then what did she know of the inner workings of a marriage? She had no experience of her own to compare it to, not even a long-term relationship. She had looked to Dale and Joy as her model of a marriage. Now it seemed there was a broken space in the perfect relationship. Kathleen wasn't sure what to think about this.

"How did the meeting with Hospice go?" Esther asked her when she got home.

"Not good. Dale doesn't want to admit Joy is dying."

"Neither do I," Esther said. "I can't stand the thought either. I can't imagine what Dale is going through."

"But what about what Joy is going through?"

"This is something they have to deal with together. It's not our place to interfere." Kathleen knew her mom was right, but refused to accept it. Surely there must be something she could do, she told herself.

Chapter 25

Mary threw her purse on the table when she got home. Tom looked up from the living room where he was reading the paper, then went back to reading.

"Aren't you going to ask me what's wrong?" Mary said as she came into the living room.

"No, but you will tell me anyway." He folded the paper and laid it in his lap.

"Hospice, they brought in Hospice. It was all that Kathleen's idea, I'm sure. She's no good, never has been."

"Now, Mary, what exactly happened?"

"Like I told you, they had two women from Hospice come over."

"Has Joy been put under Hospice care?"

"Do you even listen? No, but they are talking to them, that's almost the same."

"No, it isn't. What harm is there in talking?"

"Because, it just . . ." Mary stopped then started again. "Because we can take care of our own. Remember how I helped care for Mom before she died?"

"I do . . ." Tom started. Mary went on without hearing what he said.

"I took care of my mom and I can take care of my daughter, when and if the time comes. It's what I do. I'm her mother. I'll not have strangers looking after my baby, feeding her, bathing her. That's my job."

"No one is trying to take that away from you." Tom got up and went over to her. "You're a good mother, always have been."

Mary continued on without listening. "It's all I have. I have to protect her. Why can't I keep her safe?"

"Because we can't keep our children safe from everything," he said, putting his arm around her shoulder.

"She will not die. I will not allow it. Children do not die before their parents. We will fight this and there will be no Hospice," Mary shouted, pulling away from him.

Tom tried in vain to hug her. "It's not our decision to make, Mary, but Joy and Dale's."

"You're no help," Mary snapped. "I don't know why I even try to talk to you."

"But I'm right," Tom quietly insisted.

"No, you're not. If you need me I'll be in the kitchen fixing supper, all I'm good for." Mary stormed out of the room. Tom knew better than to follow her. He could hear pots and pans banging in the kitchen. He picked his paper back up and sat down.

Dinner was quiet. Tom made small talk. Mary sat in silence, cleaned the kitchen, sat in front of the TV without watching, then went to bed early. Tom waited enough time for her to get ready and be in bed by the time he came upstairs. He quietly joined her in bed, then held her as she cried.

Chapter 26

Joy waited till bed time to approach Dale about what had happened that morning. He had been quiet all night. Not talking much except to the kids and Lucky.

"What's going on with you?" she asked as they prepared for bed.

"Nothing, nothing's going on. Can't a man be quiet now and then? Why do we have to talk about everything? Why can't you just let some things rest?"

"Dale, what's up with you? This is not like you," Joy persisted.

"I don't want to talk about it," Dale got into bed, picking up a newspaper to read.

"But I do. I need to talk about this, especially with you." Joy climbed into bed next to him.

"It's always about you, isn't it?" Dale stated, putting the newspaper aside.

"No, this is about you. How can I help you if you won't talk to me?"

"But it is about you, Joy, it has always been about you. I don't know what I would ever do without you. I can't imagine it. I don't want to imagine it. It's not true. It's not happening."

"But it is happening, Dale, and we need to talk about it."

"Maybe you need to talk about it. I don't want those Hospice people back in my house."

"But if not, what will we do when I get weaker?"

"If you get weaker."

"When, Dale, when. We both know it's just a matter of time."

"No, we don't. I can't accept that. And I can't accept that you have accepted it, Joy. You've given up. You can't give up. You have to keep fighting this." He took her hands in his.

"Is that what you think? That I've given up?"

"Yes, why else would you talk to Hospice? Why would you even consider Hospice?"

"I thought we were in agreement about Hospice?"

"I was just going along with you. I thought it was your call. I thought this was what you wanted. It didn't hit me what it actually meant until those women came her and kept talking about dying."

"But what if I am dying? Can't we talk about it?" Dale let go of her hands and faced forward, sinking into the bed.

"No . . . I don't know. I can't talk about it yet."

"Will you ever be ready?"

"I don't know. I thought I was, back when the doctor first mentioned it. But back then it had seemed like a distant possibility. Now, with those women in our home, it's like it's here already. I can't accept it."

"But is it all right if I want to see them?"

"Joy," Dale turned to face her, "I want you to live as long as possible."

"I want that too, Dale, but at some point we have to accept the reality."

"Do we? Do we have to? Why can't we just go on as we have?"

"Because, I'm not getting any stronger. I'm getting weaker."

"No, you aren't, Joy. Fight this for me, for our children," Dale insisted.

"Okay, Dale, whatever you say," Joy agreed verbally. He fell asleep, holding her in his arms. In her heart, Joy felt alone as she lay there in his arms, seeking rest.

Chapter 27

She was standing on a cliff, looking out over a wide expanse of water. In the distance was a boat. Then she was on shore. The boat turned into a small rowboat. In the boat were her children, not as they were now, but thirty years ago. They looked so small and vulnerable as a storm brewed about them, lifting the boat on rocky waves.

Esther yelled at them from the shore, "Come in, bring the boat to shore," but they didn't hear her as the boat was carried by waves farther and farther from sight.

She rolled over and felt warm arms wrapping her tight.

"What's the matter?" the voice said.

"Kathleen and Dale. They're in trouble and I can't help."

"They'll be okay," the voice assured her.

"And you can't help either," Esther said. "Why did you leave us?"

Esther rolled over again and realized she was dreaming. The voice belonged to her husband, Dale, dead for over thirty years. She had not dreamed about him for years. Those first years after his death she would wake up as if in a dream and not believe he was gone. At times in her dreams, she would feel his arms, holding her, supporting her. She smelt him next to her, but that had stopped long ago as she came to accept the reality that he was gone. For some reason, since she had started dating Peter, the dreams had returned. She didn't know why. She felt guilty, like she was cheating on her husband Dale and Peter at the same time. Betraying Dale by dating Peter, betraying Peter by dreaming of Dale, Sr.

She had dated several men over the years, but none for longer than a few dates. She had been too busy, first raising her own children, then raising her grandsons. Peter had been a breath of fresh air, a gift. So why had Dale returned in her dreams?

The night before she had gone to Peter's home to fix dinner. He had stood over her as she cooked, offering his help, offering his suggestions. He fancied himself something of a chef.

"Hmmm," he said as she sautéed vegetables in a pan.

"What?" she asked.

"Nothing."

"I know it's something."

"Just wondering why you didn't caramelize the onions, that's all."

"Did you want to take over?" Esther offered him the spatula. They had been together long enough now, almost two years, so that Esther was able to read his grunts. He had been alone for over ten years, long enough to become set in his ways.

The first time she had cooked for him, he had not said anything. Now they were comfortable enough with each other to say what was on their minds.

She had shared her concerns about Kathleen and Dale many times.

"I don't know what's going on with Kathleen or Dale. I'm worried about Dale. I don't know how he is holding up."

"You certainly had your struggles, raising two children on your own after their father died. Somehow you managed."

"Yes, but this is different."

"How so?"

"I had no warning, no time to prepare myself. Now that I'm seeing what Dale is dealing with . . . I don't know. Neither is easy, I guess. Is it better to have time to prepare for death? If I had known what was about to happen to Dale's father, I don't know that I could have handled it."

"Like slowly pulling off a bandage or just ripping it off quickly."

"No, there's no comparison. No matter how death comes, it's hard."

"You got through it. Dale will get through it too," Peter said, reaching for her hand.

"It's so hard to see him hurting. I wish there was something I could do. I wish he were little again and I could tuck him in bed and tell him everything will be all right. Little kids, little problems . . ."

"I know, big kids, big problems." Peter had his share of worries over his own kids. He was also very aware of the problems kids got into from his years as a probation officer.

She could talk to Peter about her kids, but who could she talk to about her dreams of her late husband? Who could she talk to about

Peter? Not Kathleen. Theirs was not that type of relationship. No heart-to-heart talks for the two of them.

Most of her friends had been from her work place. A group of them met for breakfast once a month, but it wasn't the same as when they saw each other every day at work. Now it required effort to stay in touch. Not only had she lost her source of income when she had lost her job two and a half years ago, she had lost the social network that had revolved around her job.

No, she didn't know who to talk to about her love life. She went downstairs and started the coffee in preparation for another day.

"You going over to Dale's?" she asked Kathleen when she appeared at the kitchen door.

"Not today, we had our weekly visit," Kathleen said as she stirred cream and sugar into her coffee.

"How is Joy doing?" Esther asked, "Is she doing as good as she pretends to be?"

"You know Joy."

"Yes, I do, that's why I'm asking."

"Hard to say. I guess she's doing as well as she can, given the circumstances."

"I guess." They sat in awkward silence for a while, each sipping their coffee. "I'm really proud of you," Esther finally said, breaking the   silence.

"What are you talking about?"

"The way you've been helping out, helping Joy. I know it can't be easy."

"It's hard on all of us," Kathleen tried to brush the compliment away.

"I know, but Joy talks to you. I'm glad she has you to talk to."

"I don't know how glad I am."

"That's precisely what I'm saying. It's hard. She needs someone to talk to. I'm glad you are there for her. I'm sure Dale is glad in his own way."

"Enough, Mom," Kathleen wasn't going to get soft and mushy. "I've got to go." Kathleen didn't have to go, yet she did. She took another gulp of coffee, set it down and got up. She didn't want any more of this conversation, even though she appreciated what her mom had said. "Thanks," she said, pausing before going out the door.

Esther, left once again to her own thoughts, wondered at what her Dale had said. "They will be okay." Will they? If only she could believe that.

Chapter 28

It seemed that Kathleen was the only one Joy could talk to about what was going on inside her. But Kathleen wasn't enough. She called her pastor and asked if he had time to talk to her.

"Of course, when is a good time?" Pastor Joe said.

Joy arranged to meet him at his office the following morning. After Mary had encroached upon the visit with Hospice, she didn't want to take a chance on that happening again.

"Are you sure you are strong enough to drive yourself?" Mary asked. "What errand is so important? Can't I take care of it for you this afternoon?"

"No, Mom, it's something I have to do for myself," Joy told her. She was still able to drive places, just tried to do so sparingly. She was going to the studio each day, but sat during most of the classes instead of walking between dancers, making adjustments, pointing out improper positions. She left that to her helpers. She was intent on making it through this year's recital. After that was Sara's wedding. She had no plans beyond that.

"What can I do for you, Joy?" Pastor Joe said as he greeted Joy and escorted her to a chair in his office. She looked so thin, even thinner than he remembered from church.

Now that she was here, Joy didn't know where to begin.

"I don't know. I just had to talk to someone." Joe waited for her to fill the silence rather than rushing in with a question.

"I'm dying," she said finally.

He responded by taking both of her hands into his, continuing to wait for her.

"There's no one I can talk to about it. Only Kathleen. Everybody else refuses to talk about it."

"By everyone, do you mean Dale?" Joe asked.

"Yes, especially Dale. I feel so alone in this. He thinks that I've given up, that admitting I am dying is the same as giving up.

"Have you given up?"

"Maybe I have. What else can I do? I don't want to die, but I keep getting weaker. I'm tired of fighting this."

"Did you tell Dale this?"

"I tried but he wouldn't listen. He kept saying I have to keep fighting. Am I wrong, Pastor? When do you keep fighting? How do you know it's time to give in, let go?"

"What does your heart tell you?"

Joy paused to listen to her heart. Tears welled as she replied, "To let go."

Joe waited before saying, "There's a difference between giving up and letting go. I've known you long enough to know you are not a quitter. A quitter would have given up long ago."

Tears continued to glisten in her eyes.

"Tell me about your tears. What are they saying?"

Joy looked down before responding: "That I want to live what life I have as fully as possible. I don't want it to just slip by. I want to treasure every moment that I have left with Dale and the kids."

"And it's hard to do that if he refuses to talk to you."

"Yes. What can I do?"

"You can't force Dale to acceptance."

"I know. I've never been able to force Dale to do anything he didn't want to do. It's just, I've never felt he was so far away as he is now. We've had disagreements before. We were always able to work them out. But this, this is different."

"You have to let him come at his own pace, in his own time. Can you accept that?"

"I guess I don't have any choice in the matter."

"Yes, you do. You can make yourself and Dale miserable demanding he accept something he's not ready to accept – or you can let this go too, let him find acceptance in his own time, in his own way."

"A lot of letting go," Joy said.

"There's more to come. That's why we get so much practice at letting go during our life. So that when you get to that final letting go, you can do so with confidence knowing our God is waiting to catch you."

"I don't know that I believe that – that God will catch me. I mean, I believe it in my head, just not in my gut."

"The good thing is that, that is enough. Whether you believe or not, God will still be there to catch you. I just think it makes the letting go process a little easier when you have faith."

"What do you mean?"

"We all die, but not everyone dies well. You are being given an opportunity for that, to say your final goodbyes, take care of any unfinished business, tell your loved ones how much you love them, how important they are to you. Not everyone gets that opportunity. They die quickly with no time for goodbyes, or remain in denial, never accepting the reality or the opportunity it poses. Not everyone dies in a state of grace, being given time to make amends and get right with their God." Joe paused before continuing. "Dale will come around, but if not, this doesn't have to stop you from saying your goodbyes, taking care of unfinished business."

"I just wouldn't feel so alone if Dale were onboard with this."

"You aren't alone, you know that. I'm here for you, any time. Call me any time, day or night."

"Thank you, and I do have Kathleen, Dale's sister," Joy added. "She's been great help and a sounding board when Dale hasn't been." At the mention of Kathleen, Joe's ear perked up. Couldn't be the Kathleen Reese he knew from school, he told himself, then pushed the thought aside in order to continue with his pastoral duties.

Joy felt better, calmer, after talking to Pastor Joe. Dale noticed the difference immediately after he got home. He didn't know what had happened, just that he no longer felt the same pressure he had been feeling to do something – to be someone he couldn't be at that moment. Relieved, he was able to continue with his façade.

Chapter 29

Pastor Joe had seen Scott and his brother Josh at the Christmas Eve service which they had attended with their grandmother and great grandfather. Kathleen had been noticeably absent.

"Come on, Mom, if we have to go, so do you," Scott told her.

"The roof would collapse if I dared enter a church. There would be lightning bolts thrown down from the sky. It would be a disaster beyond compare," Kathleen joked.

"Ha, ha, Mom, very funny, lol." Scott had not been amused.

"It's Christmas, Kathleen," Esther said. "Couldn't you come this one time of the year? Kathleen continued to refuse.

"You go on. I'll be waiting here with Christmas cookies and eggnog."

"We'll pray for you," Erick told her as they went out the door.

"Do that. I need all the prayers I can get," she responded. At home alone on Christmas Eve, the house was empty. "I can't fake a faith I don't have," Kathleen reassured herself. She was a lot of things, but at least she wasn't phony, she continued to tell herself. Not like all those hypocrites who would be at church tonight.

She felt almost self-righteous at the thought as she turned on the TV and watched "It's A Wonderful Life."

They hadn't bothered to ask her to go to the Easter services with them. She had made her point at Christmas. Not that Scott had been that reluctant to go. He had started going now and then with his grandma, leaving Josh and his mom at home, in order to see Stephanie. Kathleen was only partially aware of the friendship. She chose to deny it, bristling whenever she saw Stephanie's dad at school events.

"You aren't hanging out with that Stephanie any more are you?" she questioned Scott.

"No, Mom, not at all," he told her, not the least bit bothered by the lie. What his mom didn't know wouldn't hurt her or him.

That was why she had been surprised at the latest phone call from the school. It seemed Scott was getting an award for his efforts to prevent bullying, along with Stephanie and two other students. The school hadn't been able to reach Esther on her cell phone because she had been in class, so they had called the home phone and got Kathleen instead.

"Are you sure that is my Scott?" Kathleen asked.

"There's only one Scott Reese in the school," the secretary said. "He's going to be recognized at an all-school assembly along with three other students. We want the parents to know so they can attend if they want. They've done a wonderful job combatting bullying this year."

Bullying and programs to combat bullying had been all the rage this year and several years earlier. Kathleen had dismissed it as yet another one of those passing fads that came and went in communities. A few years ago the school had been on a self-esteem kick. Everything had been about building self-esteem. Now it was anti-bullying. Who knew what it would be a few years from now. What the newest craze would be.

Still, it was good that Scott was being awarded for something. He was not athletic like Josh and so didn't have after school sports to keep him out of trouble or to give him something to excel at besides school. His grades were not as good as Josh's. Kathleen stopped herself there. She didn't want to be comparing the two boys, and yet here she was.

"Of course, I'll be at the assembly," she said. "When did you say it was?"

She had been surprised to see that one of the other recipients had been the dreaded Stephanie, the pastor's daughter. Maybe she had been wrong about her, she told herself. But no, she took one look at Stephanie and felt she was seeing herself in high school. No, she told herself, she couldn't be trusted.

"Congratulations on Josh getting the award," Pastor Joe had said in passing.

"Yeah, you too," Kathleen responded, not wanting to say any more.

"I thought I had told you to stay away from Stephanie," Kathleen said at the dinner table that night.

"You did," Scott agreed.

"So," she waited for an explanation.

"I ignored you," he said nonchalantly. "We're just good friends. No harm in that."

Erick laughed at this interchange.

"What are you laughing at?" Kathleen asked.

"Nothing, just seems I've heard such conversations before, at this same table, about thirty years ago." Kathleen chose to ignore the comment.

Chapter 30

"You are going to Sara's wedding, aren't you?" Joy asked Kathleen. She looked forward to their weekly visits.

"I'll be at the reception," Kathleen responded.

"No, the wedding, in the church."

"You know I haven't been in a church since I was a teenager, if you don't count the services I attended out of boredom while in prison."

"You have to come. I expect you to see me in all my glory, coming down the aisle."

"Isn't it the bride that does that? I can see you at the reception."

"Sara will be disappointed."

"She'll be okay with it."

"I'll need someone to help with Ashley and Jacob, make sure they don't mess up." Joy seemed to be enjoying this game. She finally brought out her winning hand, the kids. She knew Kathleen couldn't say no to the kids.

"Can't your mom do that?"

"Mothers of the bride don't have time to help. She'll be too busy crying."

"Then Dale."

"Dale will be busy with me and Grace." Joy smiled, knowing she had her. Kathleen reluctantly agreed.

"All right, if I say yes, will you stop pestering me about it?"

"Yes," Joy agreed. "It's all set. You'll help with Jacob and Ashley."

"Yes, I will." Kathleen felt surprisingly okay about being roped into this. Much as she avoided church, she was happy to be included as an integral part of the family, something she would not have expected a year ago. She figured she could tolerate a church service for Joy's sake.

"Are you okay?" Kathleen asked as she looked over at Joy and saw her grimace.

"I'm fine."

"I can tell you are not fine. Don't lie to me. Are you in pain?"

"I'm always in pain. It's just a matter of degree." Kathleen didn't like the sound of this.

"Isn't Hospice taking care of your pain meds?"

"Yeah, but there are side effects. I could be free of all pain but I would also be groggy or knocked out. This way is better."

"I could score us some marijuana?"

"What?"

"You know, marijuana, wacky weed, pot, Mary Jane? I could get you some. Would you use it if I did?"

Joy smiled. This hadn't exactly been on her bucket list, but why not, she thought. "Sure, what would it hurt?" she agreed.

Chapter 31

The months to the wedding had quickly flown by, especially since moving the date up to June. So much to get done with so little time. Fortunately, since moving the venue from Detroit to her hometown, her mom and sister were able to help more. Unfortunately they had to settle on the church hall for the venue, which wasn't the setting of her dreams, but her mom had assured her that, with Joy's help, she would be able to work her magic and transform the hall into a venue suitable for a fairy princess.

"Mom, really, no gauze and crepe paper," Sara said. "I mean, I'm not a kid anymore."

"Just kidding, Sara. We'll have linen table cloths and real table settings befitting the grown-up you have become."

"Thanks, Mom." Joy wasn't able to do any of the leg work for the wedding, but she was able to add her suggestions and make phone calls. She enlisted a family friend as DJ and contacted the local florists until she found one able to take on an additional wedding during this busy season. The photographer Sara had wanted from Detroit wasn't available that weekend.

"Don't worry, Sara. I know someone who can do it," Dale told her.

"Not Jake," Joy intervened.

"What's wrong with Jake?" Dale asked.

"Nothing, but he's not a professional. You want to have good pictures. It's not an area where you want to skimp. I'll see who I can find," Joy assured Sara. She was enjoying being a part of all the planning. Joy made phone calls during the week and set-up appointments for Sara for the weekend. This way they were able to pick their cake, find a photographer and hair dressers.

"I couldn't find any hair salons with space, but I've talked to my hair person and she will bring a friend and do our hair and make-up here before we go to the church."

"That'll work. I don't know how you do it, Joy," Sara said with relief. The last piece of the puzzle had been put into place.

Joy had made it through the recital by relying on a wheelchair to get around. She had sat in the wings helping with costumes and chasing dancers on and off on cue. At the end she had been rolled out onto the stage for the final bow and received a standing ovation, a dozen roses, and a basket full of cards and small gifts from her students. She had been exhausted afterwards, but only Dale saw it as she allowed the smile to leave her face and sunk into the car for the drive home. Mary was keeping the kids for the night to give Joy a break after the long day.

"You did good, kid," Dale said, affectionately reaching over and touching her face. "Tired?"

"Yes, very," Joy said. It took too much effort to smile. She had been smiling the whole evening. It felt good to no longer have to put forth the effort.

"We'll put you to bed as soon as we get home," he said.

Joy laid her head back and closed her eyes, but she didn't sleep.

"My last recital," she said, her eyes still closed.

"Don't say that. There will be more."

"Dale, who are you kidding? Not me, not anyone but yourself. I think the kids even know."

"Let's not spoil the night by talking about this."

"How does facing reality spoil the night? I think it makes it more special. This recital was more blessed precisely because I knew it would be my last. Life is all the more precious for being limited. If we never died, I don't think we would appreciate life. When you don't know if you'll ever see spring again, spring is even more beautiful."

"You are beautiful," Dale said.

"This saggy skin, hanging on my bones. These sunken eyes, you call these beautiful? I don't think so."

"Yes, because they are you, they are part of who you are. You will always be beautiful in my eyes." Joy rode in silence a while longer.

"Dale."

"Yes."

"I want you to remarry, when I'm gone."

Dale remained silent, not acknowledging her remark.

"When I'm gone, I want you to marry again," Joy stated again. "Find someone kind who will love our kids. I don't want you to grow old alone. No one should grow old alone, especially not you. You have so much love to give."

"Don't, Joy, just stop talking," Dale finally responded.

"Maybe not now, but someday. I want you to remember this conversation and remember that I want you to be happy. I want you to love again. Promise me."

"I'm not promising anything. It's not going to happen, Joy. There will never be anyone I can love like I love you."

"I didn't say you would love her like you love me. It will be a new love. Promise me."

"If it will make you happy, I promise, but it won't happen."

"It does make me happy," Joy said. "Now get me out of here and take me to bed," she said, wrapping her arms around him as he lifted her out of the car and into their home, all too aware of how light she felt. Lucky followed them upstairs and slept at the foot of their bed.

Joy didn't go to the dance studio for the last week of classes and the end-of-year parties.

"They can go on without me," she told Esther. "I've had my chance to say goodbye. My last hurrah so to speak. It feels anti-climactic to go back." She spent the day going through all the cards and gifts, treasuring each one and the love they represented as she said her own private goodbye.

"I'll explain to the instructors," Esther assured her. Joy continued to be worn-out from the recital and wanted to get her strength back for Sara's wedding. She had good days and bad days. So far the good days outnumbered the bad. Esther hoped it would continue that way.

The hospice nurse had brought over oxygen. "For when you feel out of breath," she told Joy. At first Joy hadn't wanted to use it, but when she realized how much better she felt when she used it, she stopped fighting it so much.

"The cancer in her lungs must be affecting her breathing," Esther had commented to Kathleen. She was still able to go out without oxygen, but only for limited amounts of time.

"You will be okay to attend my wedding?" Sara had asked her. Joy had sounded so tired when she had called her that week.

"Of course. I won't miss it for anything," Joy insisted. "I'm just tired from the recital."

It had been hard, saying goodbye to her students, knowing that would be her last recital. Saying goodbye to the students who had been such an important part of her life for the past ten years. How could she say goodbye? How could she bear to go back, at least not while there were still students there?

"What will happen to the studio when I am gone?" she had asked Esther and Kathleen a few weeks earlier.

"What are you talking about?" Esther had said.

"You know what I'm talking about. I don't want to see the studio closed. There's no way Dale could run it. I want you two to take over the running of the studio," she told them.

"Joy, how could we?" Esther protested.

"Leticia can teach the classes. Esther - you can manage the books, take care of pay roll. You are already doing that. You'll need to hire more instructors. Maybe Leticia can help you with that. You need someone who knows dance to run that part of the studio, but you can manage. I'd like for the studio to go on. I'll talk to Dale about it. We can transfer ownership of the building to you."

"No, I won't accept that. I'll run the place for you, but the building will remain in Dale's name. It belongs to you and your family."

"Very well," Joy had agreed. "And Kathleen, you can help."

"Of course I will," Kathleen said. They had already talked about this during one of their weekly sessions.

Kathleen was using Sara's studio as the office for her advocacy business, but she didn't need much space so far, just a desk and chairs. She was thinking about opening up a book store in the space, one specializing in healing and wellness, along with selling dance supplies, like Esther had suggested before. She and Esther had been talking about it for some time.

"It could be Joy's Gift Shop. Part of the proceeds could go to support breast cancer research," Kathleen had told Joy. "We could continue the classes for breast cancer survivors, maybe set up support groups in one of the rooms downstairs."

"Whatever you want to do." Joy had no energy to invest in something new. She needed all of her energy for what she was doing. Saying goodbye to all she had known and done over the years, saying goodbye to those she loved.

"Dale, how can I ever say goodbye to you?" she told him one night.

"You don't have to," Dale insisted.

"I love you," she whispered as they made love.

"I'm afraid I'll hurt you," Dale said. Joy guided his hands and encouraged his love making.

"I'm still here," she reminded him as they kissed.

Chapter 32

Morning showers gave way to sunshine and blue skies on the day of her wedding. Sara was nervous and excited. So many details to go wrong.

"Too late to elope?" Larry had joked the day before.

"Ha, ha, not funny," Sara responded. "We just have to get through tomorrow," she told him.

"I hope we do better than get through it. I hope we enjoy it."

"You know what I mean, right?"

"I know. I just want you to lighten up."

"I'll lighten up when everything is done and I'm at the reception dancing with you." Sara was concerned that everything go smoothly, and that Joy would be okay.

"You know there will be problems, always are. That just makes it more interesting." Pastor Joe had tried to ease her anxiety at the rehearsal. "What's important is that by the end of the day, you will be married."

His reassurances hadn't helped.

"Joy is looking so weak. I hope she will be okay."

"She'll be fine, everything will be fine. And when it's over, it will be just the two of us. I can't wait to start my life with you." Larry reassured her.

Their house wasn't ready yet, but ready or not, they were moving in.

"It will be fun," Larry insisted. "I mean, like camping but with indoor plumbing." At least the electrical work and plumbing were done. The kitchen still needed work. They would have to rely on their microwave until their new oven was installed. Still, it was manageable. Larry had been able to sublet his apartment for the remainder of their lease. They would continue to pay Sara's share of her apartment with Anne until the lease ran out. Sara figured that was the least she could do. It wasn't ideal but it worked. Sometimes Sara wondered if it had been a mistake to move the wedding up, but when she saw Joy after the recital, she knew they had made the right decision. Joy was still able to walk on her own and would be able to walk down the aisle at the wedding - but she was so weak. Who knew whether she had three months left to live, much less whether she would be up for a wedding in September? This had been right despite any inconvenience and problems.

They had decorated the hall before the rehearsal. Joy gave orders from her wheel chair, giving instructions as to what needed to be done as others did her bidding. The rehearsal went smoothly. Joy was to be the matron of honor, Anne the maid of honor. There were two more bridesmaids, friends from college. Larry had asked Sara's brothers to be groomsmen. His best friend was his best man and his brother the other groomsman. Dale was recruited as usher. Ashley was the flower girl and Jacob the ring bearer. The rehearsal dinner was uneventful as well.

Sara kissed Larry good night at her parents' doorstop.

"This will be the last night I have to say goodbye to you before going to bed," Larry said with a smile. He was sharing a room with his best man at a local hotel. The next night they would be staying together in the hotel before going on their honeymoon to a cottage up north. With all of the expenses for the wedding and their house, they had decided against an expensive honeymoon, opting to use the Lake Huron cottage of a friend of Larry's.

"Someday we'll take that dream honeymoon," Larry assured Sara. "Maybe for our twenty-fifth anniversary."

"Really? I hope I don't have to wait that long," Sara smiled. "Don't stay out too late," Sara instructed Larry as he left.

"Just a drink then bed," Larry assured her. He was meeting his friends in the hotel bar for drinks.

Sara, sleeping in her old bedroom, felt like a little girl again. She woke up to the smell of her mom's coffee. Was it possible that she was being married today, she wondered. She felt like she was back in high school. She came downstairs in her pajamas and surprised her parents who were reading the paper.

"Good morning, Sara, would you like some breakfast?" her mom jumped up to serve her.

"No thanks, Mom. I'm not hungry."

"Nonsense, you can't go all day without eating. You'll faint during the wedding."

"I can't. I've got to get over to Joy's to get my hair done. Is Anne up yet?" Anne was staying in the guest bedroom. "Besides,

Joy said she would have food for us, bagels, Danish, fruit." Sara looked at the two of them, eating breakfast together like they had for so many years, and thought how old they looked. When did they get to be so old, she wondered? They had always been older than her friends' parents, but not this old. For some reason she had never really thought about how much older they were until today. She felt small and vulnerable, going out into a new life, while the world she knew was ending.

"Mom, Dad," she said, "I want to thank you for everything."

"For what, dear?" her mom asked.

"For being such good parents, for this home. For your help with the wedding, for your help all my life."

"Just doing what parents are supposed to do," her dad said. "You sound like it's the end of the world, like we'll never see you again."

"Really, would you just let me thank you," Sara said, kissing her dad on his forehead.

"Of course, honey. You're welcome," her mom said. "And thank you for being our daughter." Sara was relieved to see Anne come into the kitchen. They both grabbed a cup of coffee then rushed over to Joy's. Sara wondered if Larry were up.

"I better call Larry," Sara said.

"Don't worry," Anne told her. "This is your day. You shouldn't have to worry about anything. I'll take care of Larry. Here, have a mimosa." Sara tried to relax and allow herself to be pampered.

The wedding was at two o'clock. They were to be at the hall by twelve to get dressed. The reception started at five o'clock giving them time for pictures and to relax before making a grand entrance.

The wedding went smoothly. Joy had been able to walk down the aisle. She stood for Sara as she came down the aisle and sat in her wheelchair for the rest of the service. Ashley made it down the aisle with little fanfare. She was a natural. Jacob was Jacob. He tugged at his suit and pouted while walking down the aisle. Kathleen sat them down next to her during the service.

As Larry and Sara exchanged vows, Joy wished she were sitting next to Dale, holding his hand for strength. She looked over at him and caught his eye. Was it possible they've been married for ten years? Seems like just yesterday. Ten years and three children later, she was still beautiful to him, Dale thought. He was even more in love with her.

Kathleen found herself wondering if she would ever find someone who would love her the way Larry loved Sara, or the way Dale loved Joy. She looked over at her sons and followed Scott's gaze across the church to where two young girls sat, Stephanie and her sister. So be it, she decided. No sense in fighting it any more. It wasn't so bad, being here in a church. It was different from what she remembered, not the church of her childhood which had been so much bigger. Still she was relieved to have the ceremony over so she could get outside.

After pictures in the church, Joy went home for a nap before the reception while the rest of the bridal party took pictures about town.

"Would you mind taking care of Ashley and Jacob until the reception?" Dale asked.

"Sure," Kathleen agreed. What else was she doing anyway, she thought. Her sons went home with her mom and grandfather while she stayed with the wedding party for pictures. When Ashley and Jacob were no longer needed, Kathleen took them to McDonald's for shakes.

"Don't spill anything on your clothes," she instructed as they sat down.

"Mom is always tired," Jacob said.

"That's because she's dying, stupid," Ashley stated bluntly.

"I'm not stupid."

"Are too,"

Kathleen wondered at Ashley. Was this the same five-year-old she had talked to two years ago?

"Who said your mother is dying?" she asked Ashley.

"Timmy Richards. He said he heard his mom and dad talking about it."

Kathleen wondered about this conversation. Had it occurred on the playground? Kids could be so cruel. She remembered being taunted on the playground. Recess was more like war in her memory. She had been taunted because her dad had died. She had tried to hide the fact, pretend it wasn't true. Kids attacked anyone who was different. Not having a father made her different. She wondered what it had been like for Dale. Was it different for boys? He never seemed to be bothered about it, not like she was.

Ashley and Jacob attended the school associated with their church, St. Luke's. Everyone knew everyone and everyone's business. Was it any wonder the other kids knew about Ashley's mom, maybe even more than her own kids did?

"What's dying?" Jacob asked.

"It's like what happened to our hamster last year," Ashley said. "Arnie went away and never came back."

"Is Mommy going to go away and never come back?" Jacob asked Kathleen. Both kids looked at her, waiting for her answer. Kathleen didn't know what to say. She looked at her phone to check the time.

"Would five o'clock ever get here?" she mumbled to herself.

"I think it's time to go back to the church," she said. It wouldn't hurt to be a little early, she told herself.

Jacob and Ashley seemed to have forgotten the conversation by the time they got to the hall. They got out of the car and made a dash for the hall, running around tables. Kathleen wished she could forget so easily. She was relieved when Sara's brother's wives arrived with their children, cousins to entertain Ashley and Jacob for a while.

"Make me your strongest drink," Kathleen told the person setting up the bar for the reception.

"We aren't open yet," he said, his back to Kathleen as he continued setting up.

"Come on, what's a gal gotta do to get a drink here?" The bar tender turned around, preparing to say "no" again, then said, "Kathleen, what are you doing here? In a church?" Kathleen recognized him from the Green Door.

"I might ask the same."

"I'm just making some extra cash."

"My brother's sister-in-law is the bride. I've been watching my seven-year-old niece and five-year-old nephew."

"Then you do need a drink. I'm afraid the selection is limited, this being a church and all."

"Scotch on the rocks?"

"No, but I've got Seven and Seven."

"That'll do." Kathleen said.

"Haven't seen you around in a while. What have you been up to?"

"Oh, you know, work, school, kids, the usual."

"That never stopped you from coming over after work before."

"Yeah, well, things have changed." Kathleen was relieved when others came up for drinks, freeing her from the need to make small talk. "I'll be back," she said, gulping her drink.

Joy and Dale arrived around five thirty, just in time for the big entrance of the bride and groom and the bridal party. Kathleen found her table and sat down as Esther, Peter, her sons and grandfather showed up. "About time," Kathleen said.

"It appears you have found something to occupy your time," Erick commented as Kathleen finished off her second drink. Kathleen didn't respond.

Their table wasn't far from the head table. Kathleen watched Joy who was barely eating the chicken which was standard fare for wedding receptions. When she saw Dale stand up and start to wheel Joy out of the room, she jumped up, grabbed her purse, saying, "bathroom break," and headed Dale off.

"Going to the restroom?" she asked.

"Yes," Joy responded.

"Here, I'll take over from here. You go back to your seat and finish eating." Kathleen wheeled Joy into the bathroom and waited in the sitting area next to the toilet stalls. When Joy came out of the stalls, she helped her back into her wheel chair and sat down next to her.

"You doing okay?" she asked.

"I'm okay, why do you ask?"

"I noticed you didn't eat your meal."

"Nothing tastes good. And I have a hard time keeping food down."

Kathleen reached into her purse and pulled out a joint. "Here, this will help," she said.

"Wait, is this?"

"The pot I told you about. You said you would try it."

"Here in the church hall?"

"Why not? There's no one else here. Everyone's busy eating. You'll feel better and it will help your appetite."

"This is crazy, but okay," Joy said. Kathleen lit the joint, took a puff then passed it to Joy with instructions. They passed it back and forth a few times.

"Who would have thought back in high school that twenty years later we would be sharing a joint," Kathleen laughed.

"Life does create strange bedfellows," Joy agreed.

"You didn't like me much in high school."

"You weren't that likeable."

"I guess I wasn't exactly Miss Congeniality."

"That you weren't." They passed the joint again.

"Ashley and Jacob asked me if you were going to go away and never come back," Kathleen said, becoming serious.

"What did you tell them?"

"I didn't tell them anything. I changed the subject. Ashley knows you are dying, another kid at school told her, though how much she understands I don't know." Joy sat with a frown on her face, thinking. "Have you talked to her yet?" Kathleen asked.

"No, I should have known this would happen. Everybody knows everybody's business at that school." Joy paused, taking another drag before continuing. "I guess I should. Dale and I should. This is something we should do together. If I can just get him to agree to it."

"Is he still in denial?"

"I don't think so, but he continues to avoid talking to me. I don't know how much longer he can keep doing that."

The door opened and Mary came in. "It's time for the first dance," Mary said then sniffed the air. "Sara wanted me to come get you. What is that smell?"

"Weed, Mom," Joy laughed.

"Weed?"

"Marijuana, pot," Kathleen explained.

"So that's what it smells like. What are you doing?" Mary asked

"It's for Joy's cancer."

"Yeah, Mom, it's purely medicinal," Joy said, laughing.

"Want to try some?" Kathleen asked. She offered the burnt stub to her.

"Of course not . . ." Mary started to say, but then thought better of it. "Why not? What will one puff hurt?" She said as she sat down and took a puff.

"I don't see what all the commotion is about. Doesn't taste like anything much and I don't care for the smell," Mary said as she took another puff.

"We better get out of here before Sara sends someone else to get us," Kathleen said, pushing Joy out, followed by a giggling Mary.

"Time for some wedding cake," Joy laughed.

"Where have you been?" Dale asked after Kathleen wheeled her back to her place. "Have you been smoking weed?" he added after catching a whiff of her hair. Joy ignored him.

"Look how beautiful Sara is," she commented.

The DJ announced the Father Daughter dance. Sara took her dad by the hand and led him out on the dance floor.

"This was a long time coming," her dad said.

"Really, Dad? I'm not that old."

"Not you, me. Hard to believe it's been ten years since I danced with your sister at her wedding. No more Father Daughter dances for me."

"Don't worry, Dad. That's why I picked one easy to dance to."

"How long is this song?"

"Long enough. You're supposed to tell me how beautiful I look."

"Didn't I already tell you that in the church?"

"And you're supposed to tell me what a great kid I was and how I'll always be your little girl."

"You were and you will," Tom responded. "I guess I'm not always good at word stuff."

"That's okay, Dad. I mean, you were good at what's important."

"And what is that?"

"Being there for us. You were always there for us as kids, going to school functions, tucking me in at night."

"That I was. I hated to miss bed time. Those times I was on the road for business, I missed bed time most."

"I don't remember you ever being gone."

"I guess that was your brothers and sister, back when I was a sales rep. Those days were over by the time you came along."

Strains of "Goodnight, my Angel," filled the room.

"That's why I picked this song, because of all those bed times, your stories and your prayers," Sara explained.

The DJ spoke over the music and announced, "The bride would like to invite her sister to join her on the dance floor in honor of Father's Day." Larry escorted Joy out on the dance floor where she joined Sara and Tom.

"My beautiful daughters," Tom said, tearing up. "Do you remember us dancing at your wedding?" he asked Joy.

"Of course, Dad. You stepped on my feet."

"I guess I was never a good dancer. Your mom loved me anyway. I don't know where you got your grace on the dance floor."

"Must have been Mom," Joy said.

"My Joy and my Sara," Tom said as the song ended. "Joy and laughter," Tom said. Sara had been named after Sarah in the Bible who had laughed when told she was pregnant. Tom always equated Sara with laughter. "You have brought joy and laughter into my life. Thank you, both," he said.

Dale came up to help Joy until the rest of the bridal party joined them for a dance. Joy danced with the best man; Dale danced with Ashley and Jacob, until he decided to cut in.

"Mind if I dance with my wife?" he said as he put his arm about Joy's waist. "Are you holding up okay?" he asked in a whisper.

"How can I not be okay when I'm with you," Joy said with a smile. "So good to dance with you," she said as the music ended. "But I think that's enough for now." She was ready to be back in her wheelchair but her feet longed to be on the dance floor. She had to be content with watching others.

She watched as her dad danced with her mom and Dale danced with Esther.

"It was a beautiful wedding," Tom said. "You did a great job pulling it off."

"I wasn't exactly alone in this," Mary said.

"I know, but you did a lot," he said as he smelled her hair. "What is that smell? Is it a new perfume? Musky. I like it."

"How are you holding up?" Esther asked her son.

"I'm fine. Just look at Joy, how happy she is."

Esther looked and saw how tired and frail Joy looked, but didn't say this to Dale. "Yes," she said instead. Dale gave his mom a hug at the end of the song and rejoined his family.

Jacob came up to Joy. "Mommy, you haven't danced with me yet," he said.

"Or me," Ashley chimed in. "Come dance with us."

"Let's all dance," Dale said, placing Grace in Joy's lap and pushing her out onto the dance floor in her wheelchair. Joy danced in place, moving as she was able in the chair, laughing as Dale whirled her around.

Kathleen wanted to dance. She looked for a suitable partner, first searching out Sara's gay friend, Jeff. She figured he would be a good dancer. Sara was dancing with him. When he wasn't available she saw Pastor Joe. He wasn't her first choice but at least he was available.

"Come on, Pastor, dance with me," she pulled him out on the dance floor. Joe hadn't danced with anyone since his wife's death. It felt good to hold a woman in his arms again, even this difficult woman. As he brushed against Kathleen's hair he smelt the unmistakable odor of marijuana.

"You've been smoking pot," he stated.

"It was for Joy. I was just keeping her company," Kathleen said.

"Sure. And where did you do this?"

"In the women's bathroom." Joe could see it already. Word that someone had been smoking pot in the church bathroom would spread throughout the congregation and greet him by tomorrow morning.

"Pastor, did you know someone smoked pot in the women's bathroom last night?" someone would say.

"Why no, how terrible. How do you know this?" he would ask and be regaled with all the details from the gossip network.

He would have to answer for it at the next church board meeting. He would be blamed for letting non-church members use the hall. The fact that it was Joy's sister would mean nothing. There will be a petition to only allow church members to rent the hall, not that that would have prevented this incident. Anyone could have brought the pot into the church. Even if it had been a church member's wedding, any one of the guests could bring in pot without him knowing. His mind raced.

"What are you worrying about?" Kathleen said. "It's not a big deal. It was just one joint. It was for medicinal purposes."

"You don't know what you have done, the consequences if this gets out among church members."

"Relax, we burned a candle to mask the smell. No one will know. Don't be so uptight." Kathleen was questioning her decision to drag him out onto the dance floor.

"Hey, Dad," Stephanie bumped into them while she danced with Scott. "Way to go," she said, giving him a thumbs up.

"Look, it appears our children are friends. Maybe Stephanie isn't such a bad influence after all," Kathleen made a conciliatory remark.

"Who's the bad influence on whom? Maybe I shouldn't let my Stephanie be friends with your Scott."

"There's nothing wrong with my Scott. In fact, I think he may have been a good influence on your Stephanie."

"Well, at least my Stephanie doesn't have a pot-smoking parent."

"No, she has a tight-ass, no fun, minister for a parent who can't even enjoy a simple dance. Excuse me," Kathleen said as she left the dance floor. Joe went in the opposite direction.

"That didn't go well," Joe thought.

"I see you were dancing with the Pastor," Joy said when Kathleen joined her.

"Yeah," Kathleen muttered.

"You looked great together. He is single, you know," Joy tried to lead Kathleen on.

"And no wonder why. When someone is his age and single, there usually is a reason for it."

"You're his age and single," Joy responded.

"And will probably stay so," Kathleen stated. She was ready to go home. "You want me to take the kids so you and Dale can stay longer?" she asked.

"No, I think I've had enough for one day," Joy said. She looked over at Dale and he went to get the kids.

"Why do we have to leave? It's not over yet," Ashley protested.

"Because your mom is tired," Dale said.

"She's always tired," Ashley complained.

"That's enough, young lady. It's your bed time. Time to go."

"Can't I stay with Aunt Kathleen?" Ashley appealed to Kathleen.

"That's up to your parents," Kathleen said, not wanting to get caught in the middle.

Joy and Dale exchanged glances. Ashley had been difficult lately. It would be easier to let her stay with Kathleen.

"Okay," Joy said. She didn't want to fight with Ashley. It felt like she was pulling away from her.

"I won't be staying too long. She can stay over with us. I'll bring her over tomorrow," Kathleen said. The kids were frequent guests at Esther's and had pajamas and other clothes there.

"She can come to church with Mom." Dale didn't want Ashley getting the idea she could skip church when she stayed with Aunt Kathleen. "Okay, young lady. You behave for Aunt Kathleen and Grandma," he told her. "We'll see you at church tomorrow."

Joy was quiet on the drive home. Dale helped her upstairs.

"I'll get the kids to bed," he told her. "You rest." Joy was too tired to disagree, but she was too wound up to sleep. She was still awake when Dale came to bed.

"It was a good day, wasn't it?" Dale said as he pulled her close to him.

"It was a beautiful wedding."

"What's wrong?"

"Ashley - I feel like she's pulling away from me."

"She just wanted to stay longer at the party. What kid doesn't want that?"

"Kathleen told me Ashley knows I'm dying."

"Where did she get that idea?"

"One of the kids at school. It's no surprise. St. Luke's is a small community. It was inevitable. We have to talk to her about it." Dale pulled away. He knew the truth of what she said, just didn't want to admit it.

"Okay," he said after a while. "I guess we have to talk to her."

"And soon," Joy insisted, "Maybe tomorrow."

"We'll see," Dale said. "We are going over to your mom and dad's after church for breakfast and to watch Sara and Larry open their presents, remember. Maybe after that." The reception had been fun. For just a moment he had forgotten about his troubles, forgotten what was never far from his mind. Now that had been taken from him. He was being forcibly reminded of that which he wanted to avoid.

"Would you do it again?" Joy asked Dale after a while.

"Do what?"

"Would you marry me again, knowing all you know now, knowing what was ahead?"

"What kind of question is that? Why would you even ask that? Of course I would marry you again, in a heartbeat. I wouldn't have it any other way. I'd marry you not despite of everything, but because of everything." Dale paused as he struggled to find the right words. "The life we share, our family, it's precious to me. Not just the good times, but the hard times too. You are precious to me. That's why I can't bear the thought of ever losing you."

Joy quietly listened to Dale. Finally she said, "I think it's time."

"Time for what?"

"I can't climb the stairs anymore. You can't keep carrying me up and the down the stairs. I think it's time to get the hospital bed, set it up in the living room." She had already discussed this option with Hospice. The bed was theirs whenever they were ready. She was ready.

"You let me decide what's too much for me. You are not too heavy for me," Dale said.

"It's too much for me," Joy said. Dale didn't know what to say.

"Is that what you want?"

"No, it's not what I want, but maybe it is what I need."

"Okay," he agreed. "We'll contact Hospice on Monday and make the arrangements, if that is still what you want to do."

"Thank you." It had not been how she had expected the night to end, not what either had anticipated, but it was what it was. It was time.

Chapter 33

Scott was having a great time at the reception dancing with Stephanie and her sister, Michelle. Josh wasn't much of a dancer.

"Why is your brother so stuck-up?" Stephanie asked.

"He's just not a dancer," Scott explained. Josh also deigned it beneath him to spend his time with his brother and another freshman.

"Not much fun?" Kathleen asked Josh. "Isn't there anyone your age here?"

"It's all right, Mom. I don't mind."

"Well, come on. At least you can dance the chicken with your mother."

"No way, Mom," Josh said in horror. It was bad enough to dance with your mom, but the chicken dance?

Esther and Peter had been enjoying the opportunity to dance together.

"It was a beautiful wedding," Esther commented as they danced.

"Yes, it was. I'm glad I was able to be part of it," Peter responded.

"And why wouldn't you be?"

"You know, it's not like I know Sara."

"But you know Dale and Joy."

"I know."

"And more importantly, you know me," Esther said with a smile.

"That I do, that I do," he responded, holding her closer as they swayed to the music.

They were on their way back to their table when Kathleen and Ashley dragged them back out on the dance floor for the chicken dance, along with Scott, Stephanie and Michelle. Kathleen looked over at Pastor Joe, standing against the wall, talking to some elderly woman and looking on. *Suit yourself,* she thought. *What a wet blanket.*

After the dance she went for one last drink before calling it a night.

"Hey, if you want to hang around after the reception is over, a gang of us will be at the Green Door later tonight. We can go together," the bartender told her.

"No, thanks. I've got my niece to take care of," Kathleen was thankful for the excuse.

"Another time."

"Sure," she said. She was bored, but not that bored.

The reception was winding down. Sara and Larry stayed for the whole reception.

"Not like my day when the couple would sneak off and leave the reception in order to get the honeymoon started," Erick commented.

Esther and Peter exchanged smiles at this.

"Last dance," the DJ announced. Sara and Larry tried to get everyone on the dance floor.

"Come on, everyone, join us," Larry said.

Josh and Stephanie were among the first on the floor.

"Come on, Grandpa," Kathleen and Ashley tried to drag Erick onto the floor.

"It's way past my bed time," he said.

"All the more reason to dance, Dad. It'll wake you up," Esther joined the conversation.

"Yes, and I'll pay for it for weeks. You youngsters go on."

"Suit yourself," Kathleen said as she and Ashley joined the rest of dancers.

"Will you dance with me?" Michelle asked Josh. He looked at her and thought better of saying no.

"Sure, why not?" he said and went out on the dance floor.

"So you can dance," Stephanie commented when she saw him.

"I guess I have to have the right partner," he answered with a grin, smiling at Michelle.

Pastor Joe joined Erick at his table.

"How come you aren't dancing?" Erick asked.

"Oh, I'm not much of a dancer. And how would it look?"

"Would probably look better than you sitting here with this old fart."

Stephanie looked over at her dad and left the dance floor to get him. "Come on, Dad. It's not like we are twerking, join us. And you too," she said including Erick in her request. "You're the only ones not dancing."

Joe looked at Erick and said, "I will if you will."

"How can I turn down such a charming young lady," Erick responded.

Erick, Joe and Stephanie joined the group on the dance floor as they formed a circle around the bride and groom. Kathleen was surprised to find herself next to Joe in the circle. She refused to acknowledge him at first, then commented, "Well, I guess you can have some fun after all."

"Couldn't say no to my daughter," he responded. He was relieved when the dance ended.

"Come on, girls," he rounded up Stephanie and Michelle and escorted them out despite their protests.

"See you," Stephanie said to Scott as they left.

Kathleen gathered Josh, Scott, Ashley and Erick and left as well. She was glad to go home.

Esther and Peter were among the last to leave. They stayed to help Mary and Tom and members of the bridal party clean up the hall. Many hands made light work and they were soon saying good bye as well.

"It was a beautiful wedding," Esther told Mary as they hugged. Mary held her close for a moment before letting go.

"Thank you," she said. She didn't have to say anything more. They both knew what was left unsaid.

Chapter 34

Joy was too tired to go to church the next day.

"You go on without me," she told Dale. "I'll be okay. Just help me downstairs and I'll stay on the couch while you go to church."

"I hate to leave you alone," Dale said.

"I won't be alone. Lucky will keep me company." Dale reluctantly agreed. Joy was relieved to have everyone gone. It was nice to not have anyone hovering over her, worrying about her. It felt free to be by herself. She lay down on the couch until Lucky barked to go out. With effort she got up, walked through the kitchen to the mud room and opened the door.

It was a beautiful morning. Joy looked out the window and longed to sit in the sun. Maybe when Dale got home she could sit outside for a while. As she watched Lucky run about the backyard, she asked herself, why not? She felt strong enough to make it down the steps. Maybe she could walk around the yard and look at her flowers.

She carefully started down the porch steps, holding onto the rail. Her slippered feet missed the last step, throwing her off balance and onto the ground. Lucky came over immediately, licking her face. Joy was embarrassed more than hurt. She hoped none of her neighbors had seen her fall. She leaned on Lucky for support to pick herself back up. She managed to make it to a patio chair, sat down and started to sob. She wasn't even sure why she was crying. It felt good, was a release. She couldn't cry like this when other people were around, except for possibly Pastor Joe.

Joe had been visiting once a week since her visit. Often they would go outside and walk in the woods as they talked until it was too much for her even with Joe's help. Then she would sit outside with Joe, wrapped in a blanket. She seemed to get chilled so easy these days. She wished she had thought to bring a jacket or blanket to cover up with as she sat, chilled despite the sun's rays. She didn't have any insulation left on her bones.

She decided against going back inside, not wanting to risk another fall. She allowed the tears to stream down her face. She didn't even have the energy to sob for long. Grieving was exhausting. Lucky lay down at her feet, covering them to keep her warm as if knowing instinctively this was what she needed.

"Good dog," Joy said as she reached down to pet him.

"Listen to the tears. What are they telling you?" Pastor Joe always told her. "Listen to your heart."

Joy didn't want to listen to her heart because it was breaking. She couldn't imagine letting go of even more. She was still Ashley, Jacob and Grace's mother. How could she relinquish that? But she knew someone else would have to take over that job for her. Who? Her own mom couldn't do it. It would be too much for her. Kathleen was good with her kids, maybe she could do it? But even as she thought this, she recoiled inside. She hated Kathleen as she thought of her, anyone, raising her children, wiping their tears when they cried. Yet if she couldn't do it, who would? Dale couldn't do it by himself.

"You know Dale is going to need help when I'm gone," she had told Kathleen last week.

"I know." Kathleen knew better than to fight Joy on this, to insist she was not going to die any time soon.

"I've read that, how kids deal with the loss of a parent is determined by how the remaining parent deals with the death." Kathleen didn't want to hear this, did not want to have this conversation. How did I end up in the role, she asked herself. She knew how, told herself she should feel honored that Joy trusted her enough to talk to her about things she couldn't even discuss with Dale. Right now though it didn't feel like an honor.

"I want you to help Dale, especially with the kids. He can't do it alone but I'm afraid he won't ask for the help he needs. He'll try to tough it out alone. That's why he needs you."

Kathleen cried internally at the thought that her brother might actually need her. She hadn't been much of a big sister. She didn't know if she could start being one now, didn't know if she could handle it. When Kathleen didn't respond, Joy continued.

"Promise me you'll be there for Dale and the kids. Promise." Kathleen wanted to run out of the room screaming. Don't make promises you can't keep, she remembered Dale telling her in high school when she was trying to finagle something out of him by promising something she had no intention of doing. She didn't remember the details. She just remembered the lies, the broken promises. How could she promise this? How could she not?

"You know, I've not been very good at keeping promises in the past, don't you? That's why Dale doesn't trust me."

"But you will keep this promise. You have to work to rebuild trust once it's broken."

"Some things are broken beyond repair," Kathleen wanted to say. Instead she said, "Okay, I promise. I'll do my best."

"That's all I ask," Joy said, closing her eyes in relief as if the effort to convince Kathleen to promise had drained her of energy.

But now, last night, even as Kathleen was doing precisely what she had asked, helping her with Ashley and Jacob during the service and before the reception, taking Ashley home with her, she felt resentful. She resented the fact that she couldn't do this for her daughter, hated Kathleen for doing what she couldn't do. She knew she was being unfair, but it hurt too much to try to be fair.

Joy remembered evenings cuddling with Ashley on the couch as they watched a video, Jacob upstairs asleep.

"Mommy, why do you have a bag of peas on your feet?" Ashley had asked.

"Because it makes my feet feel so much better."

"I want my feet to feel better," Ashley had stated. When Joy had put the peas on Ashley's feet she had squealed. "That's cold." Joy had just laughed.

"Here, help me rub lotion on my feet," Joy had said, removing the frozen peas and squirting some cocoa butter in Ashley's hands.

"That smells good. Can I put some on my feet?" Ashley had asked.

"Of course," Joy had responded, rubbing Ashley's feet between her hands and kissing them. Had it only been two years ago, she wondered. Didn't seem possible. Ashley had grown so much in only two years. It wasn't fair.

"Life's not fair," she remembered Pastor Joe saying. "That doesn't mean you have to just accept that without protest. Cry out to God at life's unfairness." And so she had cried to God, yelled at God. No one was listening.

"God is listening. He is near even when he feels far away," her Pastor had assured her. And so she had continued to cry out to God with what little she had in her until she could cry no more. She had so little energy to cry, and yet so many tears inside. Would she ever get them all out? She reached down and patted Lucky.

Chapter 35

Howard had been wanting to see Lucky, see the whole family since getting back to town in May. But something had been holding him back. He had walked through the home he had once shared with his wife. It wasn't the one they had raised their children in. Once their kids were on their own and well established they had decided to downsize into a smaller house, easier to keep clean, less up-keep and all on one floor so the only stairs they had to maneuver were to the basement. Or at least he had decided and Helen had gone along with him. The house had two bedrooms and two baths. On the rare occasion that both kids came home with grandchildren, there was a pull-out couch in the basement and plenty of floor space to accommodate children.

"We'll spend our retirement traveling, visiting our kids, seeing the world. We can visit your family in Ireland and my family in England and tour the states. There are plenty of places right here in our own country that we haven't seen yet," he had told Helen. That was before her diagnosis. They had managed the trip to Ireland and England and visits to their children's homes, but as the disease progressed it became harder and harder to take Helen any place. She became frightened and disoriented in unfamiliar places. There had already been some signs of encroaching dementia when they sold their family home and moved, but he had attributed it to normal aging. They had only been in their new home for two years when given the diagnosis.

He had felt guilty for years for moving Helen out of the home they had shared for more than thirty years to this new and unfamiliar home. He knew now the importance of the familiar for people with this disease. Their new home was filled with their old and familiar belongings. He had resisted when Helen wanted to keep old furniture.

"New furniture for a new home, a new future," he had said, but he hadn't fought her on this. "At least let's get a new mattress and box springs." She had agreed to that. As her disease progressed he was grateful for all of the treasured knick-knacks and beaten up furniture as they helped Helen hang onto memories that were slipping away.

As it became increasingly apparent that their days for travel were over, they had gotten Lucky. One of the selling points of the new home had been the fenced in back yard with room for a small garden and flowers. Helen had always loved flowers and had spoken of someday having a garden. The garden had never materialized, first because of their travels, then because of Helen's increased disorientation, but she did enjoy caring for the flowers in the backyard. The fenced-in area was perfect not just for a puppy to roam, but for Helen. As the disease progressed, Howard could lock the gate and watch from the kitchen window as Helen puttered around the back yard. He didn't need to worry about her getting lost in the unfamiliar neighborhood, wandering away and not finding her way back.

It seemed he died many deaths during that time. Little by little, the woman he loved was taken away from him leaving him with an empty shell where once had been his wife. He remembered the pain of the first time she had looked at him and not known who he was. The vacant look in her eyes. "Do I know you?"

He didn't know how he had coped, but he had. He had learned how to cope with this new reality in order to care for her in their home for as long as he could. It was only when her care became too physically demanding for him and she had slipped out of the house twice during the night in her nightgown that he had finally accepted she needed to be placed in a nursing home.

His children had supported him in this, still he felt guilty every day when he left the nursing home. He visited daily in the hope of getting one more glimpse of the girl he had married. He brought Lucky with him on these visits. Helen seemed happier to see Lucky than to see him.

"Who are you?" she would ask as long as she was still able to speak, until even that was taken from her.

Lucky had been a comfort to him as he rattled around alone in this house. That was why he couldn't imagine letting him go. But Lucky was also a reminder of all he had lost and those painful years of his wife's illness so even though it was hard to let go, it was also something of a relief. Nothing to keep him in this town now.

The months in Florida had been good. There had been plenty of widows eager to keep him company, but he wasn't ready for that, not yet anyway.

"You've still got some good years left," his sister had reminded him. "You can still travel, just not with Helen." Not with Helen, the words reverberated through his head.

That was it. He didn't know that he wanted to travel any more. Whenever he had dreamed of traveling in retirement, it had never been alone. Helen had always been at his side, his co-pilot. Without her he felt rudderless, adrift on an unknown sea and not sure where he was going. He felt free now that he no longer had to care for her, but it was a freedom he hadn't wanted or sought out. It just was. He didn't know what he wanted.

He hadn't put the house up for sale. He stayed south until Easter then started the journey north, stopping at his son's along the way. By May he was back in his empty house, still feeling unsure of what he would do.

After being back for a month, he figured it was about time he checked on Lucky. It had been a beautiful June morning. He got into his car for a drive and found himself going in the direction of Lucky's new home.

"It's Sunday morning. They won't be home. I'll just drive by. Maybe Lucky will be outside," he told himself. He pulled into the driveway, parked his car and got out. The house was empty as he expected, he thought as no one answered the doorbell. He went around back and was warmly greeted by Lucky.

"You haven't forgotten me, have you old boy?" he said, asking, "Why aren't you tied up?" Then he saw Joy sitting in the sun. Perhaps this had been why he had been so reluctant to visit. He had had his share of dying over the years. He didn't want to take on anymore, but Joy had seen him. It would be rude to just leave, he thought, so he went over and said hello.

"Howard, good to see you," Joy told him, not getting up, pointing to another chair.

"I'm back in town for the summer. The summer in Florida is too hot for me. Besides I can't leave my house empty all year. I was in the neighborhood and thought I would see how Lucky was doing."

"Lucky's fine."

"And how about you?"

"I wish I could say the same about me."

"So how are you?" Howard asked, sitting down next to her.

"Not good. I'm not doing well. The cancer has spread. There's nothing more that can be done for me. We are going to talk to the kids about it this afternoon."

Howard sat in silence for a while. "That's hard. I remember when Helen and I told our kids about her Alzheimer's, but they were adults by then. Still it was hard. It doesn't get easier, this life of ours, does it?"

"I guess not."

"Helen was Irish. She told me the Irish have a saying, 'Cry when a baby is born, laugh at the funeral,' or something to that effect."

"Why?"

"Because while on this earth there are troubles. Only in death will we be free of our troubles."

"I don't know, Howard, there are troubles, but there is joy as well, there is laughter, good times, wonderful times. I'm going to miss all of those."

"Well, that's the Irish for you. Always weeping in their beer." Joy smiled at this.

"Where are your children now?" Joy asked.

"My daughter's in Seattle. Son's in North Carolina."

"Far away," Joy said.

"They both have this idea that I should go live with them, but I'm not ready for that. I don't want to be put out to pasture before my time."

"I can understand that," Joy said.

That was where Dale found her after church. He had seen a car parked in front of the house and wondered who was here. He had gone in the front door and panicked when Joy wasn't on the couch. Then he had gone into the kitchen, looked out the window and saw her sitting in the backyard in the sunshine with Howard.

"Good to see you again," he said shaking hands with Howard.

"Good to see you, too. I stopped by and saw the missus out in the backyard. We've been having a nice chat. Time to go now," Howard said, kissing Joy on the cheek before he left.

"You'll be in my prayers," he promised.

The children eyed him suspiciously at first. "You aren't going to take Lucky again?" Ashley asked.

"No, dear, he is clearly your dog," Howard responded. At this Ashley relaxed. "But I would like to visit him now and then, if that is okay with you?"

"You're always welcome," Dale told him.

"Don't be a stranger," Joy echoed.

Howard went back home. The house seemed less empty after his visit. His children called him that afternoon for Father's day. Again his daughter asked him to come live with them. He told her he would think about it, all the while knowing he wouldn't.

Chapter 36

"How did you get out here?" Dale asked Joy.

"I managed, with a little help from Lucky," she replied. She chose not to tell him about her fall.

"Let me help you back inside."

"Please do," Joy said. She was ready to take up residence on the couch again.

Ashley was not happy about being home. "There's nothing to do here," she complained. "Why couldn't I stay at Aunt Kathleen's?" Dale and Joy both decided not to respond to this. They had also decided not to go to Joy's parents for brunch. Dale called Mary to let them know not to expect them.

"You will be missed, but we understand. It was a long day yesterday for all of us, but especially for Joy."

Dale fixed lunch then asked the kids to come into the living room.

"Your mom and I want to talk to you."

"What about?" Ashley said, not wanting to hear what she was afraid they were going to say.

"Let's wait for Mommy to tell you," he said as he corralled them into the living room.

Ashley and Jacob sat on chairs while Grace played on the floor. Joy took a deep breath then looked at Dale. How to begin?

Dale decided to take the lead. "Ashley, Jacob, you know Mommy's been very sick for some time now," he began.

"Yeah," Ashley said.

"Well, Mommy is dying."

"I know," Ashley said. "Timmy told me at school."

"Do you know what it means?" Neither child responded.

"It means Mommy will be in heaven," Dale continued, "with Jesus."

"I don't want Mommy to be in heaven. I want her here," Jacob protested.

"I'm afraid it doesn't matter what we want."

"Why not? Jesus doesn't need Mommy. We do." Dale looked at Joy for help.

"Whatever happens, you know I love you," Joy said.

"When Arnie died, we put him in a box and buried him. Will someone do that to you?" Jacob asked.

"Yes," Joy answered, "I'll be buried. But before that I will be very sick."

"But then you'll come back," he said.

"No, I won't, but I'll always be with you in spirit."

"Like a ghost?" Jacob asked.

"No, stupid," Ashley said. "She'll be gone and we'll never see her again." Ashley wanted to fight.

"Stop calling me stupid," Jacob said.

"Because you are stupid," Ashley continued.

Joy interrupted, "Here, come here, both of you. Let me give you a hug." Ashley started to cry then wiped the tears away angrily as Joy hugged them both. "I love you both so much," Joy said. She didn't know what else to say, what they could understand.

"Can I go outside now?" Ashley asked.

"Sure," Joy said. "Just don't leave the backyard."

"Come on, Jacob," Ashley said, taking Jacob and Lucky with her.

"How do you think it went?" Dale asked.

"I don't know. It's so hard to tell with kids. I don't know how much they understand. At least we've told them. Hopefully they know they can talk to us about this."

"I think it was harder on us than it was on them," Dale said.

"I don't know. Who knows what's going on in those small brains." Joy leaned back into the couch for a nap while Dale cleaned up from lunch. Joy's nap was interrupted by Sara and Larry.

"We couldn't leave without saying goodbye to my favorite sister," Sara said.

"Your only sister," Joy reminded.

"I know, right, and favorite." Sara had been concerned when told Joy and Dale weren't coming to watch them open gifts. She hoped Joy hadn't been too worn out by the wedding; she wanted to see for herself.

"We can't stay, have to get on the road," Sara said. "We just wanted to thank both of you again for all you did for the wedding."

"Yes, we've got a honeymoon to start," Larry said with a smile.

"I love you," Sara said as she hugged Joy goodbye.

"I love you, too," Joy whispered into Sara's ear. "Call me when you get back to Detroit," she added.

Sara sat in the car and cried.

"What's the matter?" Larry asked.

"I know it's not the case, but I feel like I may never see my sister again."

"We don't have to go if you don't want to."

"No, of course not. Besides, Joy would never allow it. She would be upset if she thought we changed our plans for her. She's okay for now, but thanks for the offer," Sara told Larry. "Time to begin our new life," she added. Larry gave her a kiss before starting down the road.

"What was that for?" Sara asked.

"Do I need to have a reason to kiss my wife?" Larry responded.

"Wife. I like the sound of that, husband," Sara said with a smile.

Chapter 37

Pastor Joe had been relieved that there was no negative backlash about the weed at the wedding reception. At least not so far. These things had a way of cropping up when you least expected them. He knew this from experience. It was as if church members kept these slip-ups as ammo to be brought out when they want to make a point. He didn't want to do anything to give them more ammo to use against him at a committee meeting. Still there had been no rumblings at the Sunday service. So far, so good.

"I'll stop by later this week," he had told Dale as he came out of church.

He had stayed longer at the reception than he had planned. Usually he would make an appearance, then be gone before any serious partying could take place. He found having the pastor around sometimes hindered the festivities. However, Stephanie and Michelle had been invited and were having a good time so he stayed for their sakes. Even though it was a short walk to the rectory from the church hall, he didn't want to leave them unsupervised. He had enjoyed his conversation with Sara's friend, Jeff, and the rest of Sara's friends who had been seated at their table.

Joe had not been surprised when Joy didn't attend church that Sunday. He knew how much the wedding had taken out of her, perhaps more than anyone because of their weekly conversations. He had been surprised at how much weaker Joy was when he visited later that week. She had a hospital bed set up in the living room, although she was dressed and still walking around the house. It was as if the wedding had been all she had been living for, the last item on her bucket list. Now that it was over, she either didn't have any reason to keep going, or had finally allowed herself to feel just how tired she was from this disease.

Hospice had brought the bed on Tuesday. She still wasn't quite ready to give up the bed she shared with Dale, but it was nice to have the bed available for naps during the day. It seemed the naps were becoming longer and more frequent. Then at night she would sleep fitfully, waking up repeatedly. Joy feared she was keeping Dale awake.

"Like I could sleep if you weren't in bed with me," he told her when she worried about keeping him from sleeping.

Joy felt strong enough to sit outside but not to walk around as had been their custom. Lucky sat at her feet as they talked.

"Where are the kids?" Joe asked.

"Kathleen took them to the park. I didn't want our visit to be disturbed," she said. Joe waited for her to continue.

"We told the kids on Sunday, or at least we attempted to tell them. I don't know how much they understood."

"They will understand as much as they are capable of understanding, much the same as adults."

"You've been through this, haven't you?"

"What do you mean?"

"The loss of a spouse. How did your wife die?"

"It was a car accident. It was sudden and unexpected."

"So not entirely like what Dale is going through."

"No, there was no chance to say goodbye. She died with plenty of unfinished business."

"I guess I should be grateful."

"I don't know that I would say that. Who would be grateful for prolonged pain and suffering? At least Janice didn't suffer long. She died instantly."

"But she never got to say goodbye to her loved ones."

"Yes, but I think that's harder on the ones left behind than the one leaving."

"I don't know. I'm glad I have this time." Joy brought herself back from this digression to her original thought. "You will help Dale when this is over? You know what it's like to lose a wife."

"Of course, I'll help Dale as much as I can. That's a given. But the circumstances are different."

"How so?" Joy asked.

"I wasn't a very good husband."

"Why do you say that?"

"Because I wasn't. On the night she died, we had had a fight. She was going to file for a divorce. She said I loved the church more than her and the girls."

"Did you?"

"No, but apparently I wasn't good at showing it. I let church responsibilities take precedence over my home responsibilities. I thought I was being virtuous, the good pastor, when I left home repeatedly for every church emergency. I took Janice for granted, figured she would always be there but then she wasn't. She never quite accepted being a pastor's wife."

"It is a responsibility."

"One she didn't know she was accepting when she married me." Joe wasn't sure why he was telling Joy this. He had not told anyone. Everyone thought he had the perfect marriage, one befitting the perfect pastor. "But this is supposed to be about you, not me."

"I'm sorry," Joy said, ignoring his last statement. "I didn't realize."

"Nobody does. I did a pretty good job of keeping this a secret."

"What a burden," Joy said.

"Nothing like your burden," Joe tried to deflect the attention away from him and back to Joy. "It's my burden. We all have our burdens. What about your burdens?"

"But you help so many others with their burdens. Who helps you?" Joy wasn't letting it go.

"Sometimes church members like you. Thank you for listening," Joe said as he prepared to leave.

"You will help Dale, won't you?" Joy requested.

"Of course," he said as he left. He hadn't wanted to go in this direction, yet it had felt comforting to know that someone besides him knew his own personal tragedy.

Joy was asleep in the hospital bed when Kathleen returned with the kids. Lucky was lying alongside her, sleeping as well. Kathleen panicked when Joy didn't wake up immediately upon their return.

"Joy, Joy, we're back," she said, sending the kids into the kitchen. "I'll be there in a minute. I just want to check on your mom," she told them.

What if she were dead? What if the kids found her dead one morning? Kathleen found herself worrying. She didn't want to be the one to find her. She reassured herself that Joy was still breathing then went into the kitchen to fix lunch.

Esther and she had both received their associate degree in May at the end of the semester. She was thinking about going on for her bachelor's at a local college, but was taking the summer off from classes. Esther was done as well and not planning on taking more classes. This freed them up to help more with Joy's care. Joy's kids were regular guests at their home. Between the two of them and Joy's mom, there was always someone around to be with Joy while Dale was at work. Josh and Scott helped as well, entertaining the kids. The thought that one of these times Joy could fall asleep and not wake up haunted her. She didn't want to be the one to find her. Esther was going to be coming over in the afternoon to relieve her before she went to work.

Kathleen was relieved to see Joy's eyes open when she came back into the room after lunch.

"What can I get you to eat?" she asked.

"Nothing, I'm not hungry." Joy had stopped eating a day ago.

"You have to eat something to keep your strength up."

"Do I" Joy asked, "Why?" Kathleen ignored the question.

"What sounds good? You can have anything your heart desires."

"Can I?" Joy said with a smile. "Everything except what I really want." Kathleen ignored that statement as well.

"How about ice cream? Just think, you can have all the ice cream you want, with toppings. How about it?"

"I think I could take a little pudding," Joy finally said. "Lemon custard."

"That's my Joy," Kathleen said but when she came back into the room with the pudding Joy barely took a spoonful.

"I guess I'm too tired," she said.

"That's okay," Kathleen said, "Maybe after your nap."

"Yes," Joy agreed, "After my nap." Kathleen walked away with tears in her eyes.

"How is she?" Esther asked when she came to relieve her.

"She's not eating," Kathleen said. She couldn't wait to get out of there. She didn't know how Dale did it.

"I'll see if I can get her to eat something," Esther said.

"I wish people wouldn't walk around me whispering like I'm not here." Dale and Esther were surprised when Joy said that. Esther had been telling Dale how Joy wasn't eating. Joy's eyes were still shut, even as she spoke. It was too much effort to open them.

"Well, now that we know you are awake, I can tell you. You haven't eaten anything today."

"I haven't? Are you sure? Seems like I just ate." Joy's eyes remained shut.

"I'll take over from here," Dale said. He sat down next to her and said, "Joy, you have to eat. Try some pudding."

Joy opened her eyes and smiled. "You are so good to me, always have been."

"You are good to me, too. Now just eat something, honey."

Joy took a small spoonful but that was it.

"I'm sorry, Dale. It just won't go down." Dale had been told about this problem already by Hospice.

"As the end nears she will sleep more and more. Eventually she will stop eating. It's all part of the natural process of her body shutting down."

Dale hated sleeping alone. He couldn't stand the thought of Joy being all by herself during the night, so when she was too weak to sleep upstairs, he started sleeping downstairs on the couch. That way he was there if she needed anything.

"How can I say goodbye to you?" Joy said one night.

"You don't have to say goodbye," Dale told her.

"I've said goodbye to so many things and people, even the kids. But how can I say goodbye to you?"

"How can I say goodbye to you?" Dale said in response. "You are my life. It's like I'm saying goodbye to life itself."

"No, you shall live. I want you to live. It's me who has to say goodbye, but not yet," Joy whispered.

"Not yet," Dale repeated, climbing up on the bed to hold her as she slept.

Chapter 38

Sara woke during the night, the last night of her honeymoon. She reached over and felt Larry, softly snoring beside her. She moved in closer and his arm came over her, wrapping her in protective warmth.

She had been dreaming. She couldn't remember the dream, just that it had something to do with Joy. Much as she was loving this time alone, just the two of them, she knew it was time to come back to reality. She didn't relish the thought of what lay ahead of her, but she knew she couldn't avoid it.

"You okay?" Larry whispered, holding her close.

"Just thinking about Joy."

"Do you want to leave early and go see her?"

"No, but thank you for suggesting it. I mean, I'll call her when we get home." Home, to their home, the home they would create together. She liked the sound of that. "We still have a day of honeymoon left. No reason to cut it short," she said as she turned in his arms and kissed him.

The honeymoon had been a wonderful escape, but the reality of Joy's situation was waiting for them. Sara called her mom for daily updates. She didn't want to be bothering Dale or Joy but had to know. When she heard Joy was no longer eating she feared it wouldn't be much longer. She arranged for time off of work. Joy tried to tell her she was being foolish, but she didn't have the strength to argue.

"I'll stay in the kids' room," she had told Dale. Much as he didn't want to impose, especially since Sara was so recently married, he was grateful for the assistance.

"Thank you," was all he said. Sara hated to be away from Larry. She was just starting to adjust to life with him, sharing their bed. She missed him all day, but especially at night. She called him each night to update him on Joy's situation. He had come on the weekend, sleeping with her on Ashley's twin bed, but they couldn't afford to have both of them take the time off of work.

"I miss you," Sara told him when he suggested taking time off, "but there's really not much for you to do here. I'll call you if that changes." So Larry had gone home to Detroit, alone, to their new home. He wandered around the empty home, fixed himself a sandwich then settled down to a night of TV watching before going to bed.

The hours by Joy's side seemed to drag on forever, leaving Sara alone with her thoughts. So many memories from her childhood, how she had looked up to her big sister, how Joy had stayed with her when she had chicken pox and their mother had to be gone, taking care of her own mother.

"Do you remember when I had chicken pox? How you took care of me," she asked Joy when Joy woke up.

Joy smiled softly, her eyes closing. "That was when Grandma died, wasn't it?"

"Yes, Mom had gone to help take care of her."

"Like you are doing now," Joy said.

"Really? Hadn't thought of it like that," Sara responded. "I was just remembering what a good sister you were."

"I had good material to work with," Joy said as she slipped back into sleep.

"I wasn't that good," Sara said quietly. "You were always the good one," she told Joy but Joy was already out. Sara continued even though Joy wasn't awake. "You were the best sister I could have had. Do you remember summers at the beach? You got stuck watching me when you would have much rather been with your friends. Remember how I followed you around?"

"I remember." Sara was startled to hear her mother's voice. "You idolized Joy. You were so lost when she went away to tour with the ballet. I was a poor substitute," Mary said. "What will we do without her?"

"Mom, how long have you been here?"

"Not long. Are you ready for a break? I brought over sandwiches."

"I'm fine, Mom, really."

"I know you are. It won't hurt you to take time out to eat. I'll stay with Joy. She'll be here when you are done," Mary assured her.

Sara reluctantly left the room, not believing her mom.

Chapter 39

"How long can this go on?" Kathleen asked. She didn't know how much more she could take. It had been two weeks since Joy stopped eating. A day since she had drank any fluids. Family members took turns coating her lips with ice chips, wiping her brow. The room smelled of death.

"I can't stand to see her this way," she added.

"It could be any day now," the Hospice nurse had told the family. She also instructed them what to expect. Joy's brothers and their wives had been over to visit on Sunday. Sara helped with all of the day to day care, helping her mom bathe her sister. She sat at the foot of the hospital bed and rubbed cocoa butter on Joy's feet.

"I remember sitting up with you when you came home from touring with the ballet and watching you put packages of frozen peas on your feet," Sara said to Joy even though she didn't respond. "And then you would talk me into rubbing cocoa butter on your sore feet while we caught up on each other's lives. Good memories . . ." Sara said looking for any sign that Joy had heard her. She thought she saw a slight smile on her lips.

"Here, let me do that," Dale said, coming into the room.

"I don't mind. I like doing it," Sara insisted.

"I know. Now it's my turn." Dale had his own memories of rubbing Joy's cracked, sometimes bleeding, sore feet. So many nights when she was still performing. Joy had loved the sweet smell of the cocoa butter and the rich feeling on her feet. She continued to treat herself to the lotion even when she was no longer performing and was not being as hard on her feet. Dale reached up and rubbed her hands and arms as well, till the room smelled of cocoa butter.

Dale only went into the office when absolutely necessary, or when shown out by his mom and Kathleen, relishing the time he had with her.

"Go on, it will do you some good to get out of here," they told him. The kids were splitting their time between their grandparents' homes, as requested by Joy. She hadn't wanted them to see her like this.

"I want their last memory of me to be a positive one." She had kissed them and told them how much she loved them, then said goodbye.

Someone was with Joy all the time. Lucky spent most of his days lying in the living room, close to her bed. Dale continued to sleep on the couch in the living room. They played all her favorite dance music during the day.

"Dale?" Joy startled him awake that morning. "Why are you here?"

"Why shouldn't I be here? This is our home."

"Oh, so it is," Joy seemed disoriented. "Would you call Pastor Joe?"

"Of course, honey. What do you want me to tell him?"

"Just that I want him to come. He'll know what it's about."

"Okay," Dale said. Joy grabbed Dale's hand as he prepared to leave.

"Tell him not to rush. We have time."

Dale called Joe, waking him out of a fitful sleep.

"Joy told me to call and ask you to come. She said you would know what to do."

"That I do, Dale. I'll be over right away."

"She also said not to rush. That you had time."

"Okay, then I'll be over in an hour or so, as soon as I've had a chance to shower and shave. You might want to call other family members."

Dale woke up Sara who had been sleeping in the kids' room and called Esther. She had been planning on coming over that morning anyway. "And bring Kathleen," Dale said as an afterthought. The kids were at Mary and Tom's, so he didn't call them.

Dale, Esther and Kathleen were all gathered in the kitchen when Pastor Joe arrived. Sara had stayed with Joy.

"Thank you for coming," Dale said, grasping Joe's hand with both of his hands. Kathleen didn't look at him. She wasn't sure exactly why she was here. She just knew that Dale had said she was to come. Was this what it would be like to keep her promise to Joy, she wondered. Come whenever he needed her?

"Often, a day or so before a person dies they get a burst of energy. I liken it to the burst of energy many women experience before they give birth. Joy is preparing for her re-birth," Pastor Joe explained.

Kathleen didn't like how this was shaping up. She wasn't interested in a lot of God talk, not even for Joy.

Joy was sitting up, alert and smiling when they came into the living room.

"Good to see you, Pastor," Joy said.

"Good to see you, too. What did you want me to do?"

"I want you to pray for me, and for my family." Joy reached for Dale's hand. Sara came to the other side of the bed and took Joy's other hand. Esther moved in next to Dale. Kathleen didn't know where to stand, hanging to the back of the room.

Joe stood next to Sara and motioned to Kathleen to stand next to Esther. He pulled out a small prayer book and began to read from it. He made the sign of the cross over Joy as he read the prayers. Then he read a passage from John's gospel, chapter fourteen, "In my Father's house there are many mansions."

Kathleen felt tears sliding, unbidden down her cheeks. Sara and Esther were dabbing their eyes. Pastor Joe invited them to hold hands and pray the Lord's Prayer. Kathleen vaguely remembered the words from her Sunday school days but they refused to come out. She couldn't bear to say them so she remained silent. Esther, Sara, Dale and Joy mumbled through the prayer, led by Pastor Joe. Then Joe prayed additional prayers for Joy, asking comfort for her family and a peaceful death as she passed from this life into the next.

Kathleen couldn't bear it any longer. She abruptly let go of Esther's hand and left the room.

With the final "Amen," Joy looked at Joe and smiled. "Thank you, Pastor, you can go now." That was Joe's cue to slip aside and leave Joy to her family for what time she had left.

He went into the kitchen, looking for Kathleen. He wasn't sure what to say but felt he had to find her and make sure she was okay. He looked out the window and saw her sitting in a chair, crying, the same chair that Joy had sat in while talking to him two weeks ago.

"Are you okay?" he asked tentatively.

"Of course I'm not okay. Do I look okay? My best friend is dying and you ask if I'm okay."

"Do you mind if I sit down?" Joe asked, pulling up a chair next to   her.

"No one's stopping you," Kathleen said, refusing to look at him.

"I know it's hard," he said tentatively, reaching for her hand. Kathleen pulled back.

"What do you know about hard? You and that God of yours."

"I know what it is to lose someone."

"Well, this isn't the same."

"No two deaths are alike."

"All that talk of God's will, God's will be done. Crap! What kind of God would will for a mother to leave her children, or a father to leave his children?" Joe was aware of Kathleen's loss through Dale. "A monster God, that's what kind. I spit on your God," Kathleen said, spitting on the ground as she continued to cry.

"What kind of God indeed," Joe said quietly. "A God who knows what it is to be human. Who knows what it is to lose a father and to die a painful death."

Kathleen didn't want to hear this. "Don't talk to me about your God. I don't believe in your God."

"Then what do you believe in?"

"I don't know. I just know what I don't believe in."

"That's a hard way to live a life, not believing in anything."

"Well, it's worked for me so far."

"And how has that been for you? It doesn't seem like it has been all that great." Joe was aware of her time in prison.

"It's been fine. It's been okay. I've gotten along. Until now. I can't believe I'm losing the best friend I ever had, maybe the only real friend I've had."

Joe didn't know what to say. He knew anything he would have ordinarily said in such a situation wouldn't work. Words like, you'll see her again in the next life. He couldn't say this to one who didn't believe. Finally he ventured, "She will live on in your memory."

"Lot of good that will do her children when they cry at night for their mother and she's not there."

"But you can be there for them."

"It's still not the same."

"No, it's not the same," Joe agreed. "I'm sorry, Kathleen. It seems all I have to give you is not enough. All I have is my faith, my words of faith, poor though they may be. I don't know how to comfort someone who doesn't believe in God. I can't imagine going through this life without faith and the help and comfort that comes from faith.”

“Maybe I don’t need you or your God.”

“But what about your God, not my God, but yours? What does God look like to you?”

“Right now, God looks like a monster who takes good people in their prime, puts them through incredible suffering and then leaves their children orphaned.”

“That’s not my God.”

“Then what is your God?”

“My God holds us in the palm of his hands. My God doesn’t keep us from all suffering in this life but is there to walk through this life with us. He is with us in all our pain. My God is holding Joy even now as she says goodbye. My God is also holding those precious children. And he’s holding you like a loving Father.”

“I wish I could believe that,” Kathleen said, her head resting on her hand as she gazed at the ground.

“I wish you could too. I’ll pray for you.”

“You do that.” Joe looked at his phone and realized he was late for an appointment. “If you ever want to talk, you know how to reach me,” he said, reaching for her hand then pulling it back as Kathleen refused to look at him.

When Kathleen went back into the living room she was surprised to hear her mother, brother and Sara all talking with Joy like it was any other day. Joy sounded like her old self. Joy smiled at her as only Joy could smile. Then she asked about the kids.

“They’re at Mom’s” Sara said. “Do you want me to have Mom bring them over?”

Sara called her parents and let them know what was happening.

“Your mom wants to see you,” Mary told Ashley and Jacob while she dressed Grace.

“Good,” Jacob said, “I want to see her.”

Ashley wasn’t so sure but knew she didn’t have an option. When she had last seen her mom, she hadn’t looked like her mom at all. When they arrived home, Jacob raced to the living room to see his mom, climbing on the bed. Dale took Grace out of Mary’s arms and held her until Joy was ready for her.

“Careful, Jacob, Mommy is a little weak,” Joy said as she hugged him. “Where is my big girl?” Joy asked. Ashley hung in the back of the room behind her grandfather. She hesitantly came forward, afraid of what she would see. Her mom almost looked like her old self. If only she would get out of that bed, she thought.

"Hi, Mommy," she said.

"Come here and give me a big kiss," Joy said. Ashley gave her mom a tentative kiss, catching the slight smell of cocoa butter, then pulling back.

"Are you being good for Grandma?"

"As good as gold," Mary said.

"Remember you have to set an example for Jacob and Grace. You're the big sister. And help your dad." Ashley shook her head yes, then slipped back to Kathleen, taking her hand.

The kids stayed for a while longer then Kathleen took them outside so Joy could have some time with her parents. When Joy started to show signs of being tired again they all went home except for Sara. Sara left Dale and Joy alone.

"All gone?" Joy asked.

"Yes, it's just you and me now. Sara's staying over in case we need her."

"Just you and me, kind of how all this started, how it was when we first got married," Joy said with a smile. "Those were good years. It's been a good life."

"Yes, it has."

"Dale . . ." Joy started.

"You know you don't have to say goodbye. Not to me. You don't ever have to say goodbye. I'll be here till the end."

"Thank you. Thank you for today. Thank you for our life together," Joy closed her eyes and went to sleep.

Her breathing was labored throughout the night. At times Dale heard the rattling sound made by mucus gurgling in her throat. The Hospice nurse had showed him how to suction it out. He didn't want to sleep but finally Sara came in and took over for him.

"You've got to get some sleep," she insisted.

He went upstairs where he fell asleep immediately from exhaustion.

Sara treasured these moments with her big sister in the early hours of the morning. Sara said her own goodbye and prayed, glad to have the time alone with Joy.

Kathleen went home to her own bed but couldn't sleep. She remembered what Joe had said, about God holding Joy in the palm of his hand. If only she could believe that, it would be so much easier, but she couldn't. She imagined Joy being held in a loving embrace by some being she couldn't comprehend or describe. She didn't believe but she wanted to believe and that was enough. She finally fell asleep with this vision in her head.

She woke up about five o'clock. The vision was still there, only this time the being took on a human form, the form of a man, the Jesus she remembered from Sunday school. Slowly, she saw him stand up, holding Joy in his arms. Slowly he walked away. Kathleen tried to cry out. "Wait!" she wanted to say but the words wouldn't form in her mouth. "What about me?" she finally asked. The man stopped, turned and looked at her with love in his eyes, then continued walking.

Dale was dreaming. Joy came to him in his sleep, not the Joy he had left downstairs, but the young girl he had fallen in love with so many years ago, the young woman he had married, the mother of his children. She was all of those at once. She smiled at him and invited him to dance with her. He held her close, relishing the smell of her body against him, until she pulled away. "I'm okay," she said as she left. "I'm not in pain."

He woke, holding on to the memory, not wanting to ask what it meant.

Sara was holding Joy's hand, her head bowed in quiet prayer when she heard Joy's breathing change slightly. Joy sighed. Her breath left her body and Joy was gone. Sara cried as she touched her sister's cheek, looking for any sign of life, waiting to see if this had been yet another false alarm, waiting for her to breathe again. When Joy failed to revive, she realized she needed to get Dale but couldn't move just yet. She couldn't bring herself to leave Joy's body.

For some reason, she wasn't surprised when Dale came into the room.

"I'm sorry, Dale. It just happened. I meant for you to be here."

"It's all right. I was here, in my dreams." They sat in silence for a while before calling anyone. The room was a sacred space. They wanted to hold onto Joy's spirit for as long as possible.

Chapter 40

"Two times in less than a month. Is this getting to be a habit?" Pastor Joe asked Kathleen as she came out of church.

"You know the only person who could get me to go to church was Joy. Don't expect to see me any time soon."

"Well, it's good to see you, even under these circumstances. We seem to have gotten off on the wrong foot. Maybe we could try again, maybe even be friends?"

"Maybe," Kathleen said. She moved on as there were others waiting to talk to the pastor.

She had not been surprised at all when they received the phone call Friday morning.

"She's gone," Dale said.

Kathleen heard Esther ask, "Do you want me to come over?" She waited for the call to be over to confirm what she already knew.

"No, Sara's here with me. We're waiting for the funeral director. There's not really anything to do right now."

"Are you sure there isn't anything we can help with?"

"Maybe with phone calls, but there's no need to do that just yet."

"I'll come over around noon. I'll bring lunch. We can figure out what else needs to be done then," Esther said as she hung up.

"Joy's gone," Esther said to the family members that had gathered in the kitchen.

"I know," Kathleen said.

"How did you know?" Scott asked.

Kathleen did not want to share her dream. "She just didn't seem like she would make it another day when we left last night."

Joy and Dale had worked out the details of the funeral with Pastor Joe and the funeral director before her death. There was not a lot to do but follow through with Joy's instructions.

Dale called Joy's mom. "Do you want me to bring over the kids?" Mary asked.

"No, might as well keep them there for a while longer. Nothing they can do here."

He had discussed with Joy whether to let the kids attend the funeral or hire a sitter.

"What I've read is that it's better for them to be a part of everything rather than ship them off to a relative."

"Can't we let them decide what they want to do?" Dale asked.

"Grace's too young. I don't know about Jacob or Ashley either. I think we better decide for them. I think that's too much to put on someone so young. What do you think is best?"

"I don't know if there is a best way to handle this," Dale responded. "I attended my dad's funeral. It is not a good memory. All I remember is the casket and Dad lying in it while everyone was crying."

"But wouldn't it have been worse if you had not gone at all?"

"I don't know. I was so young. I hardly remember my dad at all."

"Like Grace. She won't remember me," Joy said.

"We'll remind her of you. We'll tell her about you. Don't worry, you won't be forgotten," Dale assured her.

Joy didn't smile. She tried to focus on the job at hand. "It also says it can help if the kids have a memory book," Joy said reading from a booklet Hospice had provided her. "Maybe Kathleen could do that with them. Or my mom."

Dale put Sara and Mary in charge of putting together picture boards with photos from all aspects of Joy's life, from childhood, through teen years and into adulthood. It gave them something to do and a chance to reminisce as they went through pictures together.

Kathleen helped Jacob and Ashley with their memory book. Each drew pictures for their mom.

Jacob wanted to see his mom at the visitation while Ashley stayed to the edges of the room, not wanting to see this body that had been her mom.

There was a constant stream of visitors, students, former students, parents of students, church members, Dale's employees, friends from school, as well as family. Howard Jones joined the throngs, awkwardly offering his condolences to Dale then looking for a familiar face. Mary rescued him, giving him a hug and introducing him to Tom.

Josh and Scott had not wanted to attend the visitation. "What do we do?" Scott asked, "Just stand around?"

"Pretty much," Josh had said. They stood self-consciously in the back of the room until joined by other students from their high school where they clumsily tried to make conversation. A number of girls that Josh knew had either been students at his aunt's studio or still were. Stephanie came to support Scott. Michelle had insisted on coming as well.

"Scott's my friend, too," she assertted.

"You hardly know him," Stephanie had objected.

"Let her come if she wants," Joe had intervened. Michelle made a face at Stephanie.

Dale stood uneasily towards the front of the room, greeting guests, shaking hands, giving and receiving hugs, as people viewed the body and told him how natural she looked. Kathleen didn't think Joy looked natural at all. She looked like but a shadow of the woman she had known. Joy had aged years over the past months. Kathleen avoided that part of the room, sneaking off to the side rooms where there was food for the family. She found Ashley and Jacob there.

"Are you two doing okay?" she asked. She looked over at Josh and called him to her. "Can you take Jacob and Ashley outside for a while?"

"Sure, Mom," Josh was happy to get out of the visitation room. "Come on, squirts," he said, picking up Jacob and taking Ashley's hand. Jacob squealed as Josh carried him out. Kathleen looked for Grace. She was hanging onto her grandmother Mary.

"You want me to take her off your hands?" Kathleen asked.

"That would be good," Mary said. She was busy meeting family and friends. It was a relief for her not to have to watch Grace and a relief for Kathleen to have an excuse to leave.

The fresh air felt good. She kept Grace occupied for as long as she could then she decided it was time to leave.

"Do you want me to take the kids?" she asked Dale.

There were still well-wishers coming in the room, mingling. He figured he would be here for a while yet.

"Yes, if you would," his eyes looked tired yet grateful.

"Any time, little brother," Kathleen said with a hug.

The funeral had been packed as well. The whole service was a blur to Kathleen, unaccustomed as she was to being in church. There was music, prayers and tears. The pastor gave the eulogy as part of his message as there was no family member who felt up to doing this. He talked about Joy's life, sharing stories he had gleaned from family members and friends over the past few days. His concluding comments echoed the words of the apostle Paul.

"Paul tells us there are three gifts that matter, faith, hope and love, the greatest of these is love. Joy had all three but most of all she had the gift of love. She loved others and was loved in return, as evidenced by the outpouring of support the family has experienced over the months of her illness. Family members and friends visited, sent cards, flowers, brought over food, helped with her care. I know Joy would want me to thank all of you for her. Thanks to all of you for coming today and being a part of a life that ended far too soon." Pastor Joe paused and looked at his notes before beginning again.

"The greatest of these is love. Joy loved to dance. The only things she loved more than dancing was her God and her family, her children, Ashley, Jacob, Grace, and most of all her beloved husband, Dale. Now, because of her faith, because of her love, she is with her greatest love, her God in heaven where she is no longer in pain and where she is able to dance once again, and where she will watch over her loved ones on earth, her husband, children, parents, and other family and friends, until we join her in the heavenly dance."

Kathleen cried despite herself.

This was followed by a dance by some of Joy's students. It truly was a celebration of Joy's life. The celebration continued during the funeral luncheon. Kathleen found herself in line next to Pastor Joe. At a loss for what to say, she finally said, "Thank you for what you said today."

"What was that?"

"That Joy was dancing in heaven. Even though I don't believe, I still felt comforted by the words."

"Scripture has a way of doing that," Joe told her.

"Yeah, well, I'm still not going to church."

"I wouldn't expect you to," he said with a smile as he filled his plate. "Even Joy would roll over in her grave if that happened."

It was late afternoon before everyone was gone. Family members gathered at Dale's and shared some of the casseroles that had been brought over by friends.

Kathleen, Esther, Sara and Larry were the last to leave. They gathered around the kitchen table after everything had been cleaned up. Larry had come for the weekend and stayed with Sara at Dale's. He had taken Monday off from work to attend the funeral but needed to get back to work the next day. Sara was going to stay one more day before returning to Detroit and work.

"I can stay longer, if you want," Sara had told Dale.

"No, the kids and I have to get used to our new life. We have to find a new normal," Dale told her.

"What's going to happen to Joy's studio?" Larry asked.

"I guess that's up to Kathleen," Dale said.

"What do you mean?" Kathleen asked.

"Joy wanted you to have the studio."

"I told her no."

"And you know Joy. Once she sets her mind on something." Dale remembered Joy's words to him when they had discussed the dance studio. He had questioned her when she said she wanted Kathleen to have the studio. "I thought you wanted Esther to have the studio."

"Kathleen needs it more. She needs something more, something to give her life meaning. She needs to know someone believes in her. I believe in her. I want her to have the dance studio."

"And what if Kathleen doesn't want the studio?"

"She wants it, she just doesn't know that yet," Joy had insisted.

"I can't take this," Kathleen said. "The studio, it belongs to you and the kids. I'd be taking this from your kids."

"Actually, it belongs more to the bank than to me. There is still a large mortgage on the building. It's an expensive building to run. The studio hasn't been profitable for years."

"What do you mean? Joy said she was making money. It was important to her that she was contributing to the household income," Kathleen protested.

"She was, it just wasn't enough to pay all the bills and see a profit."

"Wait, how did this happen?"

"Well, at first, after that first year, the studio made a profit. But then the building became available to buy. Joy was the only tenant at that time and the owner wasn't making a profit, knew the building needed repairs and didn't feel up to doing everything that would be required. So he put the building up for sale. Joy and I decided that it would be a good investment so we bought the building." Dale took a breath before continuing. "Joy continued to pay the same amount in rent she had always paid and I took care of the rest. What she didn't know was just how expensive it was to keep heat and electricity in that building."

"Joy didn't know this?" Kathleen found this hard to believe.

"No. I figured that eventually Joy would want to quit, especially after Jacob was born. I thought at that time we could sell and get our money back. But, as you know, that didn't happen," Dale sighed. "It made her so happy. I didn't have the heart to tell her. And then, once she got sick, it gave her something to live for, something besides me and the kids. I couldn't take that away from her."

"Wow, little brother, you kept this from your wife all these years? I guess there is some of me in you after all. What other secrets do you have?"

"None that you need to know," Dale asserted. "Anyway, if you still want to take on the dance studio, given all of that, it is yours. If not, I'll put the building up for sale. No-one would blame you." Dale went to his briefcase, pulled out some papers he had on the building and handed them to Kathleen.

Kathleen looked over at Esther. She remembered how much Joy wanted them to keep the studio going.

"What do you think?" she asked her mom.

"I don't know. I guess we can crunch the numbers and see if we can make it profitable," Esther said.

"And I'll help in any way I can," Sara said, eager to be part of keeping the studio going.

"How can you help from Detroit?" Kathleen asked.

"I could still provide art work for the studio and for sale. I mean, you would make a percentage off every item I sell. I know it doesn't sound like much right now, but it could amount to something," Sara offered.

"I'll think about it," Kathleen said. And that she did.

Chapter 41

Kathleen tossed and turned all night, thinking about the dance studio and the building it was in. Could she make a go of it, she kept asking herself. There would be the added expense of hiring dance instructors to replace Joy. Her own small start-up was not yet profitable, but she would need an office, couldn't run it out of her mom's home. And there were all those dreams of opening the book store, gift shop, in the building. Maybe this was meant to be.

When she finally gave up the effort to sleep and went upstairs into the kitchen, she found she wasn't the only one who couldn't sleep. Esther was sitting at the kitchen table in front of her laptop with papers spread out all over the table.

"What are you doing?" Kathleen asked.

"I couldn't sleep. Numbers kept going through my head. I finally decided I wouldn't be able to sleep until I got them out of my head and into the computer. What are you doing?"

"I couldn't sleep either. So what did you come up with?" Kathleen poured herself a cup of coffee and sat down next to Esther.

"It doesn't look good. It costs so much to provide heat and lights to that building. I can't believe that Dale has been subsidizing the cost all these years. In order to be profitable we need to use the building more effectively. We need to fix up all those rooms and find paying tenants."

"How many do we need?" Kathleen asked.

"At least three or four others."

"Does that include an office for my business and a gift shop?"

"No, that's in addition to those. It will be awhile before those are profitable. We need paying tenants as soon as possible."

"Any prospects?"

"No, I don't know of any people right now."

"It can't be just any renters. We want renters that will buy into our vision of the place." Kathleen was beginning to get caught up in the possibility. Maybe with renters, she thought . . .

"And what is that vision?" Esther asked.

"I don't know right now," Kathleen said, "but I will eventually."

"Even if we use what's left of the insurance money from your dad's death, it won't be enough."

"So it's not possible." Kathleen felt her gut sink at the thought, like she had swallowed a ball of knots. She hadn't realized that she had started to get her hopes up, something she never allowed.

"No, I guess not," Esther agreed.

Heaviness hung upon their hearts at the thought. Tired though they were, neither wanted to go back to bed. There was nothing to do but start their day.

"I guess I better call Dale and let him know," Kathleen said.

"You don't have to do it right away. There's no rush."

"No, but I'd like to put it behind me. Besides, I'm going to have to figure out what to do about my business," Kathleen said.

"And I guess I'll need to start job hunting again," Esther said. Kathleen made no move for her phone but continued to sit at the kitchen table until going downstairs to get dressed.

Esther got the painting of Joy out of her bedroom where she had placed it for safe-keeping. She was meeting Sara at the dance studio that morning to return the painting and let Sara get the other pictures. It only seemed right that the art work go back to the artist.

"Do you want to go to the studio with me? I'm meeting Sara there at ten before she goes back to Detroit," Esther asked.

"Sure, why not. I've got nothing better to do." Kathleen agreed, glad for a reason to not call her brother just yet.

Sara was waiting for them in the parking lot when they arrived. Esther carried the picture, wrapped in brown paper for protection.

"Have you made a decision?" Sara asked Kathleen as she unlocked the door.

"Yes," she said. "I don't see how we could ever make a go of it."

Sara didn't respond. All three walked quietly through the building, none breaking the silence. It felt like they were walking on sacred ground.

Sara walked into the main room of the studio, followed by the others. Finally she broke the silence.

"I can't believe she's gone," she said.

"Me neither," Kathleen said.

"She was so happy here. I can still see her leading her classes, talking to her students, encouraging them. She loved it so much." Sara paused and looked around the room. "I can't stand the thought of losing this building too," she said with tears.

"I know, but what are we to do? None of us have the money needed to make it happen," Esther said.

"Well, let's get you those pictures," Kathleen said, looking for an excuse to leave the room. It held too many memories from the past year that she didn't want to revisit at that point. Kathleen and Sara left the room.

"You go on ahead without me," Esther said. "I'll be there in a minute." Esther remembered those nights, waiting for Joy, pregnant with Grace, still dancing despite her swollen body and swollen feet. She couldn't believe it was all over. She could see her, feel Joy's presence. Joy never gave up. How could she give up on her now, she thought. She joined Sara and Kathleen who were taking down the series of sketches Sara had drawn of Joy during her senior year in college.

"We can't give up so easily," Esther stated.

"What do you mean?" Kathleen asked.

"Joy was not a quitter. She was a fighter. We need to fight for all she created. This studio was so important to her." Esther looked over at the office where Joy's logo was displayed—Joy's Studio of Dance: Dancing for the Lord—it said. "Remember how we came up with that tag-line and the mission statement?" Esther asked Sara.

"I do," Sara responded. Kathleen had not been part of that particular adventure.

"We can't just let it end, not without giving it a try," Esther insisted.

"What do we have to do?" Sara was onboard.

"I don't know. I guess we start with the dance studio, letting students know it will remain open," Esther said.

"I can make phone calls," Sara said.

"What do you think, Kathleen? Joy wanted you to have the building," Esther said. Sara stopped talking, realizing Kathleen had not said anything yet.

Kathleen remained silent. It was all foolishness as far as she was concerned. Her brain told her not to do it. Then she remembered talking with Joy, Joy telling her how she needed meaning and purpose in her life. Maybe this was precisely what Kathleen needed most. Maybe this was why Joy wanted her to have the building. She wanted to walk away, walk away from all of the responsibility, from all of the pain, from her life here. Instead she walked into the main room of the studio.

"I don't know. Let me think about it," she said, leaving the others behind.

"I can't do it," she found herself saying to the empty room.

"Yes, you can. I believe in you." It felt like Joy was there, talking to her.

"But I don't believe in myself," Kathleen said.

"That's okay. I have enough faith for both of us," Joy reassured her.

"What if I fail? What if I make a mess of things?"

"What if you don't try?" Joy countered her argument. "The worst thing that could happen would be that you sell the building later, rather than now."

"No, the worst thing would be if I let everyone down." While this silent dialogue went on, Sara and Esther sat in the office, sharing memories, avoiding mention of the one thought that weighed on both of their minds.

"Do you think we should check on her?" Sara asked after a half an hour had passed with no word from Kathleen.

"Give her a little more time," Esther said, as Kathleen appeared in the doorway.

Kathleen didn't wait for them to ask, but burst out. "I know it's crazy. It's impossible. I don't know how we can do it . . . but I'm in." As she said it, the heaviness she had experienced earlier seemed to lift. She was still tired, was still grieving, but she felt a strange peace about the decision. Her brain continued to tell her it was crazy, but her heart said to go for it.

"Follow your heart," she remembered Joy telling her one time. Kathleen wasn't sure exactly who or what she had been following before this for all those years, but clearly that hadn't been working too well. It might be a good idea to try something new.

"It looks like we'll be needing those sketches for awhile yet after all," Esther said. "You don't mind do you, Sara?"

"Of course not." Sara and Esther put the framed sketches back onto their spots on the wall.

"And I guess this painting will not be finding a new home in Detroit," Esther said, pulling the painting out of the brown wrapping.

"Not any time soon," Sara agreed. They hung the picture back onto its prominent place on the wall in the hallway.

"It looks at home there," Esther said.

"It does," Sara agreed.

All three paused and looked at the picture, still sad, but somewhat comforted.

"So, I guess that's it," Kathleen said in the car on their way home. Esther and she had said good bye to Sara, sending her on her way to Detroit. "I guess the only thing left to do is tell Dale."

Dale was surprised to receive the call from Kathleen. He had thought she would take more time before making a decision. He was staying home with the kids. Much as he loved Sara and all of Joy's family and his own family, he was ready to be alone with the kids. They needed to figure out who they were as a family without a key member.

"Okay," Dale said. "Are you sure?"

"No, I'm not, but I'm going to try anyway," Kathleen said. "I'm going to do this for Joy."

"Okay, I'll take care of the paperwork transferring ownership to you."

"No need to rush," Kathleen said. "Do it when you have time."

Dale didn't know what he thought about this outcome. He wasn't happy or relieved. He just felt numb. There was still so much of Joy in their home. Clothes in the closet and dresser that needed a new home. He guessed he could take them to Goodwill, but not today, not just yet. They still smelled of Joy.

The hospital bed had been removed by Hospice on Friday. The room had been overflowing with guests over the weekend. It felt good to be just the five of them minus one.

He made the effort to heat up left-overs for lunch and again for dinner, finding some relief in the ordinary acts of daily life. Somehow he had to keep putting one foot in front of the other. He put Grace to bed then cuddled on the couch with Ashley and Jacob, watching a video. He didn't see the video as he sat there, his arms around his children. They, too, were reminders of all he had lost, reminders of Joy's presence. Lucky lay in the place where Joy's bed had been.

"I miss Mommy," Jacob said. "When is she coming back?"

"She isn't coming back, stupid," Ashley responded. Dale chose to ignore this remark.

"I miss her too," Dale said.

"Will I ever see her again?" Jacob asked.

"She's never coming back," Dale responded.

"Never is a long time," Jacob said.

"I know it is, but Mommy is still with you in your heart," Dale said, pointing to Jacob's heart.

"I don't want her in my heart. I want her here," Jacob said.

"Me too, son. Me too." Dale agreed and hugged him and his sister tight.

Chapter 42

Another Thanksgiving. Dale had insisted on having Thanksgiving dinner at his home.

"It's what Joy would have wanted," he had said. Esther and Kathleen took care of everything but the turkey. That was Dale's responsibility, that and making sure there were enough chairs for the crowd.

Dale had rumbled through the cupboards in search of Joy's large roaster for the turkey, climbing on a stepstool to reach the highest cupboard. When he finally found it and pulled it from its hiding place, he was surprised to see an envelope addressed to him in Joy's handwriting. Dale reached for a chair to steady himself and sat down before reading the letter.

My dearest Dale,

If you are reading this, then you are getting ready for Thanksgiving dinner as I knew you would. I always loved Thanksgiving and having everyone in our home. I don't know if I will have one more Thanksgiving with you. It will take what little energy I have to pull out the roasting pan, put this letter in it and push it back. I want to thank you one last time for all you have meant to me over the years. You were my high school love, my only love. Even though we are separated by death, I will always love you.

Kiss the kids for me, every day. Remind them of how much their mommy loves them and that I will be watching over them always.

Tell everyone who comes for Thanksgiving how much I love them all and how happy I am that they are here together. Be sure to hug Sara and my new brother-in-law, and all of the family for me, mom, dad, your mom, Michael and David, everyone.

And tell Kathleen, thank you. She'll know why.

With all my love,

Joy.

"Daddy, what's wrong?" Ashley surprised him. Dale folded the letter, wanting to keep it to himself for a moment longer.

"Nothing, Ashley."

"Then why are you crying?"

"I just miss your mom," he said. "Look what I found in the turkey roaster," he decided to show Ashley the letter.

"Is it from mommy?" Ashley said hesitantly. "Does she say anything about me?"

"Just how much she loves you and that she will be watching out for you from heaven." Dale hugged her. Ashley squirmed, not sure how she felt about this.

"Can I see the letter?" she asked. She couldn't make out all the words, but recognized the faint scent of her mother's body lotion on the envelope. "It is from her," she said with a slight smile.

With Leticia's help, Kathleen had found another instructor and the dance studio was operational. Besides the yoga instructor, she had one paying tenant. It wasn't enough, but it was a start. She figured she would give it a year.

Howard hadn't gone back to Florida to stay with his sister for the winter just yet and hadn't wanted to fly out to see his daughter so they invited him to join them for dinner. He played with Lucky and the kids while the rest of the group either helped in the kitchen or watched football. Dale had invited Pastor Joe as well. He had become like one of the family throughout the struggles of the past year.

"Thank you for the invite, but I'm taking the girls to the in-laws for Thanksgiving. You know how it is," he said and Dale agreed. He knew about in-laws. They were still family even when the person who had originally brought you together was gone.

Peter helped in the kitchen, showing some culinary skills by making the gravy.

There was an unspoken sadness as all remembered the person who was missing, yet much laughter as well and much to be grateful for. Dale told everyone about the letter, only reading that part that was for everyone.

"So, Kathleen, what did Joy mean?" he asked.

"Hell if I know," Kathleen stated.

"Kathleen!" Esther stopped her, looking over at the children.

"Who knows what Joy was thinking, right?" Kathleen continued, ignoring her mom, wanting to keep those words from Joy to herself for her own private reflection. "I'm the one who should be thanking her," she added.

Once the guests were gone and the kitchen cleaned up, Peter, Dale, Larry and Kathleen joined Sara and Esther in their traditional bottle of sparkling wine.

"So how is the dance studio coming," Larry asked Kathleen, now that they had a moment of quiet.

"It's going," Kathleen said.

"It's more than going," Esther interjected. "Kathleen's business is growing, we have an additional tenant and there's some interest in Sara's artwork."

"Yes, but we've got the Christmas recital coming up. I don't know the first thing about putting on a dance recital."

"That's why we have Leticia. She'll take care of the dances and costumes. I'll take care of the business aspects, like ticket sales, and you worry about promotion."

"Whoa," Peter intervened, "Let's not get started on business tonight." He had already heard this discussion many times.

"Yeah, sorry for bringing it up," Larry added.

"There's a reason why we hadn't invited the men in the past," Sara said.

"Yeah, who said you men could be part of our party?" Kathleen asked with a smile.

"I guess we can take our bottle of sparkling wine and go," Peter said, taking the extra bottle he had brought for the occasion.

"No, don't go," Esther said. "It's good to have new traditions, mixed in with the old. Joy would approve."

"Yes, really, she would," Sara said, sipping her glass of wine as all remembered the one who wasn't there but whose presence had dominated all day.

"It was a good Thanksgiving," Kathleen said quietly.

"Just as Joy would have wanted it," Dale said. "I don't know that I will do it again next year, but this year was good."

"Yes, this year was good. Who knows what the next year will bring," Kathleen said. "Time enough to worry about that another day."

They sat in silence till Kathleen proposed a toast. They raised their glasses and toasted each other, saying, "To Joy."

"The last enemy to be destroyed is death." 1 Cor. 15:26

Discussion Questions

1. In *Still Dancing* each character deals with Joy's terminal diagnosis in different ways. Which character do you relate to the most? Why?

2. Has someone close to you died? Have you or someone you loved had to deal with cancer? How was that situation similar to the one in the book? How was it different? Did it change you, and if so, how?

3. Are there any words of comfort you can offer to someone in this situation? What seemed helpful and what was not helpful.

4. Kathleen struggles with how she sees God. Why? Have you struggled with your image of God? If so, why, and has that changed over time. How do you see God now?

Note to the reader:

Did you enjoy reading this book? If so, please leave a review on Amazon. Your comments would be appreciated and mean so much to me in terms of helping others notice my book. You, the reader, have the power to make or break a book in this day of emarketing and social media.

Thank you so much for reading *Still Dancing*. Stay tuned for the sequel!

Patricia Robertson

Other novels by Patricia M. Robertson

Dreamweavers – Dream again, wherever you are in your life. An exploration of how our dreams change over the course of our lifetime. Join Kate, a single mom, her teenage daughter, Terri, and others as they seek out new dreams for their life.

Buying Time – Visit the peace movement during the Cold War era of Ronald Regan, SDI (Strategic Defense Initiative) and MAD (Mutually Assured Destruction). Join a rabble-rousing Catholic priest and Methodist minister, a kindergarten teacher, and a Quaker homemaker, as they beat swords into plowshares, or in this case, hammer on a B-52 bomber. Arrested and jailed, they bought the world time through doing time

Land of Deep Waters - Honduras, land of deep waters, a country torn apart by civil unrest, violence and poverty: Is it possible to go back? Thirty years after being banned from Honduras as a young nun, Joan, now married with two grown sons, finds herself haunted by memories of her four years there. She is determined to return, but how, and if so what will she find?

Magnificent Failure - Is it possible to start over? He is a Wall Street executive who drops out, leaving behind his family and livelihood in search of redemption. She is a divorced single mom, struggling to have a life of her own while raising her children. Failures in the eyes of the world and their own eyes, they found each other.

Dancing on a High Wire - What do you do when life knocks you off balance? Sara is looking forward to starting her life with her fiancé when he breaks off the engagement. Joy is expecting her third child when she is diagnosed with breast cancer. Esther is planning on continuing at her current place of employment until retirement when she finds herself unemployed with few job skills. Each needs to find a "new normal" and regain their balance on this high wire we call life. First in the Dancing through Life Series.

A Slow Waltz – The road to healing from loss is a slow one, sometimes going backward and sideways before going forward.

Sometimes the biggest barrier to healing lies within us. Join Dale, Kathleen, Ava and others as they journey to forgiveness and healing.

Robertson also is author of a companion non-fiction book to *Still Dancing*, *Walking With Families through the Dying Process*, as well as other non-fiction books, a weekly blog and monthly newsletter. She has a Doctor of Ministry and over thirty-five years of experience in ministry to families. For more information about her ministry go to www.patriciamrobertson.com.

A Slow Waltz

Chapter 1

Ava was breathing harder and harder as the cool fall air burned through her lungs. She wanted it to burn away all her memories, free her mind of all the events of the past years. After the week she had had, all she wanted was some space far away from the demands of her world, especially her classroom. She could not tolerate one more pimple-faced pubescent boy, burping and farting in the back of her classroom, eliciting giggles and groans from those around him. She couldn't tolerate her life. It wasn't the life she had dreamed of back when she had been a pubescent girl herself.

With each step her head felt clearer as she left behind her problems. This was to be a new beginning, a fresh start in a new place. Why then did her problems cling to her like a bad haircut?

She loved running. While running, her life seemed manageable. She felt capable and competent, able to take on any challenge. So unlike her true self. She rounded the path, leaning into the curve and willing her body to go faster. Finding this little bit of woods on the outskirts of town had been a godsend. She hadn't asked who it belonged to, didn't want to know, wanted to remain in blessed ignorance, assuming it was public property. Certainly God knew she needed this, a place where she could get away from prying eyes and all their questions. She needed this and God had provided so she wasn't going to question.

Her heart rate increased, pounding in her chest as she continued up the path, heading to the clearing she knew was ahead. She allowed her body to bend to the curves in the path, willing herself forward until she reached the top of the rise. It wasn't a mountain view, not like in her home state, but it still afforded a panoramic view of the town she now inhabited. She missed being able to see for miles at a time. In contrast, all of the rolling hills and forests of her new life felt claustrophobic, like they were closing in on her. Even the smells of the woods were different from the mountain air, surrounding her in a stuffy mist. But it also was a good place to hide.

She breathed in deeply, hands on knees as she bent over. A tree branch snapped behind her. She looked up and an ugly brown mutt in a bright orange vest ran up to her and attempted to lick her face.

"What?" Ava backed away, not trusting the bull dog face, crinkled as if in a grin, and the wagging tale that carried his body along with it. How dare he intrude upon her space?

"What are you doing?" The dog was followed by . . . a pimple-faced boy, or at least that was what she had thought at first glance. A second look revealed that he was older than her eighth-grade students. A youthful face appeared under a hunting cap, his body enveloped in a large hunting jacket, a rifle cradled in his arm.

"Don't you know enough to stay out of the woods during hunting season?" He removed his hat and wiped his brow, revealing that he was even older than her second guess. "At least wear something bright orange to let hunters know you are not a deer. I could have shot you."

He looked her up and down in her black running pants and brown sweatshirt.

"Sorry, I thought this was public property."

"No, this is private property, my property. You are trespassing."

"I'm sorry. Where did I go wrong? I started at the park."

"You crossed into my property at the first rise. It's clearly marked."

"Well, I won't make that mistake again, thank you." Ava turned and began her run down the hill, her face crimson.

"Wait," the hunter called after her, holding his dog by the collar lest he follow after the departing figure. Too late. She continued down the path.

Dale shifted his rifle, squatting next to his dog, and rubbing Lucky's head as he watched after her. He hadn't meant to sound so rude. It wasn't like him. But then he didn't know what was like him any more. He didn't recognize himself, hadn't felt like himself since Joy had left.

It had been over a year since she had died. It still didn't seem real. She had been so much a part of his life. It was hard to remember a time when she hadn't been there. They had known each other since grade school. He got up each day, put one foot in front of the other, took care of the kids and went to work, but he was only half alive. Everywhere he looked were reminders of his wife, sights, sounds, even smells. So much had died with her. He believed in the resurrection. For every death there is a resurrection. Where was his, he wondered as he stood up and continued to watch the path that had held the young runner.

"Lucky," he whistled. The brown mutt had wondered off into the brush. He scampered back through the underbrush, covered with burrs.

"Some hunting dog you are. You scare away the deer with your chasing everything in your path, real or imaginary." Dale was just going through the motions of hunting. It was more about being out in nature than shooting a deer. The mustiness of fallen leaves invaded his nostrils, wiping away reminders of his former life. Here, in his woods, he was alone with his thoughts in a way he couldn't be in his home. There were too many traces of Joy in their house, the home they had built together. He thought about selling the house, but what about his kids? They had lost their mother: Must they also lose their home? So he had decided against it, at least for a while.

He wondered about the woman he had startled in the woods as he turned in the opposite direction toward home. He hoped she made it back out of the woods safely.

Ava made a quick retreat. Even this small escape was being taken from her, she thought as she ran, anger rising into her throat and then swallowed down. What right did she have to be angry? She was only getting what she deserved.